the
joy
of
sheds

the

joy
of
sheds

Frank Hopkinson

PORTICO

First published in the United Kingdom in 2012 by
Portico Books
10 Southcombe Street
London
W14 0RA

An imprint of Anova Books Company Ltd

ISBN 9781907554513

A CIP catalogue record for this book is available from the British Library.

10 9 8 7 6 5 4 3 2 1

Printed and bound by Everbest Printing, China

Research: Ilyas Deshmukh
Illustrations: Damien Weighill
Cover shed illustration: Jean and David Stiles (www.stilesdesigns.com).
The shed appears in *Sheds: The Do-It-Yourself Guide for Backyard Builders*

Picture credits: Pages 67, 70, 101, 103, 107, 112, 119, 120, 121, 123, 131, 135, 138, 141, 142, 143 and 145 courtesy of Rex Features; pages 52, 60, 61, 84, 85, 92 and 94 Corbis; pages 18, 30, 56, 58, 77 and 114 Getty Images; pages 14, 17, 90, 91 and 100 Library of Congress; pages 34 and 149 Mirrorpix.

This book can be ordered direct from the publisher at
www.anovabooks.com

Contents

Introduction

Supermodel Linda Evangelista once said, "I can do anything you want me to do…as long as I don't have to speak." Leaving aside the fact that this is most men's idea of a fantastic relationship, it's also a quote that is applicable to sheds. The shed version of it would be more like, "I can be anything you want me to be." Sheds are the utility player of the outbuilding team, they can play anywhere on the park. Most of the time sheds are places where you store stuff. They are the repository of garden tools, the lawn mower, a bike or two, some gardening chemicals you vaguely know how to administer (that have gone hard after the damp got in), plus sundry insects and the occasional scuttling rodent.

But further investigation of the kind of activities that go on in sheds has revealed that there is a whole universe of activity going on in sheds around the world from Sydney to Sydenham. The first popular documentation of the men-in-sheds phenomenon was knocked together by Aussie Mark Thomson who published *Blokes in Sheds* in 1995, followed by *Shed Stories* in 1996. The Australian men-in-sheds movement is big news down under. Aussie Mens' Sheds are actually self-help groups of men banding together in sheds and passing on a whole variety of hands-on skills while enjoying the company of other men. In the UK, men are a lot more singular about their shed pursuits and, with less space in cramped suburban gardens, the sheds are significantly smaller and unable to accommodate a couple of mates as well as a scale model of the Snowdon Mountain Railway.

With the media alerted to the rich diversity of shed structures via websites such as Shedblog.co.uk and Shedworking.co.uk, hardly a week goes past without a new purpose being found for a shed. They are routinely used as bars and pubs, but to that you can add the roles of museum, tattoo parlour, (mock) signal box, cinema, diner, Roman temple, shrine, recording studio, artwork, boat, pirate ship, bowling alley and in one American example, the bridge of the *Starship Enterprise*.

This book is far more than a tour of interesting sheds that have spent too long in the dressing up box. It is a celebration of all things shed, a tribute to their versatility and adaptability, including the great roles sheds have played in world history and in creating multi-billion dollar businesses such as Hewlett-Packard and IKEA. Without his shed, Ingvar Kamprad (the I.K.

of IKEA) would probably still be milking moose on his farm in Elmtaryd, Agunnaryd (the E.A. of IKEA).

Sheds helped Marie Curie carry out important research on radiation, they helped Daimler and Benz create two groundbreaking engines, and they helped Momofuku Ando perfect the pot noodle. Which is ironic when you consider how many are consumed inside sheds today.

Sheds have played a vital role in the development of world literature. George Bernard Shaw would retreat to one each day; Phillip Pullman wrote some of his best stuff there, while Virginia Woolf and Roald Dahl couldn't write anywhere else. Dylan Thomas's "wordsplashed hut" looking out across a romantic sweep of the Taf estuary is a sight of pilgrimage for many fans and still open to the public.

Sheds are also inextricably linked with crime. A recent survey reported that 10% of owners do not lock their sheds and that shed crime is on the increase. For someone who has never locked a shed in his life that is a surprising statistic. I've got to say no-one has ever shuffled up to me in a pub car park and whispered, "Wanna buy a lawn edger?" Or, "I've got an extendable implement that can be used to snip off apples that are too high to reach by hand – a fiver and its yours." One of the shed manufacturers we contacted while compiling the Shed Facts chapter told us that a lock on the shed door is no deterrent. Apparently if a villain thinks that you've got something "tasty" in your shed then half the time they'll heave the roof off and go in that way. The good news is that your lawn rollers are probably safe.

Sheds are a big staple in comedy shows. Whereas silent movies would wreck a piano for comedy effect and *Top Gear* likes to inflict terminal damage on caravans and Morris Marinas, the next best thing to destroy is a shed. So many more would have been disposed of in all those ropy *Starsky and Hutch / Dukes of Hazzard* car chases of the 1970s except they would have been out of place. Because their natural habitat isn't at the side of the road or behind downtown warehouses they had to make do with an unfeasibly high number of large empty boxes to knock aside.

Sheds are also the subject of one of the sketches in the first *Monty Python* series where we were introduced to classical composer Arthur 'Two Sheds' Jackson. Arthur (played by Terry Jones) is a composer who has written a new orchestral work and all the interviewer (Eric Idle) wants to do is talk about his nickname. "Actually, Graham and John wrote it," Terry Jones told me before gracefully turning down the opportunity to write a foreword to this book in the persona of Arthur 'Two Sheds' Jackson. The humour may have dimmed over the years, but it has inspired men of a certain age to give the moniker 'Two Sheds' to anyone with two sheds; or just one shed who is thinking about getting a second. I had a neighbour who was a chartered accountant, who thought himself very grand and went off to talk accounting at his Masonic Lodge. When I discovered that he'd erected a second 6 x 4 foot apex shed in the corner of his garden, he immediately became known as 'Two Sheds'.

I could tell that it irked him to have "Afternoon, Two Sheds!" shouted over the fence on a Sunday, but he wasn't going to admit it. When it came to Christmas I would get the children to paint pictures of two sheds covered in snow and send it to him as a Christmas card with "Happy Christmas Two Sheds" daubed on top. He moved in the end, but he left the sheds.

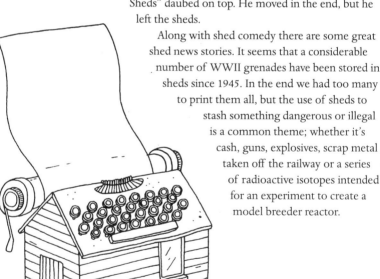

Along with shed comedy there are some great shed news stories. It seems that a considerable number of WWII grenades have been stored in sheds since 1945. In the end we had too many to print them all, but the use of sheds to stash something dangerous or illegal is a common theme; whether it's cash, guns, explosives, scrap metal taken off the railway or a series of radioactive isotopes intended for an experiment to create a model breeder reactor.

Then there are the shed facts. Because 52% of the UK population have one, everyone loves a shed fact. *Nuts* magazine and Cuprinol have produced interesting surveys on shed use and shed aspirations, but Australia's Bankwest went one stage further in 2009. They asked a series of detailed questions about shed use for their Shed Index. This comprehensive bit of shed research revealed that 11% of Australians spend more than five hours in their shed every week and that 2% of their partners resent it. When it came to modern conveniences, 7% had a computer in there, 16% had put in a TV and 27% a bar fridge. When asked if their shed 'is a refuge from the world?' 28% said yes.

They also posed the intriguing question 'What is the proudest achievement you've built/created in your shed?' Disappointingly, 37% of the population hadn't created anything useful in their shed – so they were very much on a par with artist Tracey Emin. The controversial British artist created several self-portraits in her Whitstable beach hut and then dismantled it and put it on display as a work of art in 1999.

In a similar vein, artist Simon Starling purchased a rural shed in a field, supposedly made a boat out of it to float down the Rhine and then re-assembled it, by which time it had become a work of art: one good enough to win the Turner Prize in 2005. You'd have thought he would have entered it in the *Practical Woodworking* awards as well, the job of fashioning those irregular, straight, knot-ridden timbers into a watertight hull must have been immense. And given the scale of that particular task it's surprising that so few photos exist of the really hard bit – the boat.

Many artists have used sheds as a canvas, but Claude Monet and Damien Hirst have a link in common in that both have painted in sheds. Monet stuck one on top of an open boat so he could paint the Seine river near Paris while Damien has one he retreats to at his Devon farm. It's the shed that none of the sheep go anywhere near.

All these treats and many more lie in store for you in *The Joy of Sheds*, a compendium of anything and everything sheddy. It was assembled in the spirit of a typical shed erection. If you think that some of the chapters may be in the wrong order that's because we ignored the maker's instructions and just bolted what looked to be the right sort of pieces together as we went along. Frankly, you're lucky to have this introduction so close to the front.

Frank Hopkinson, 2012

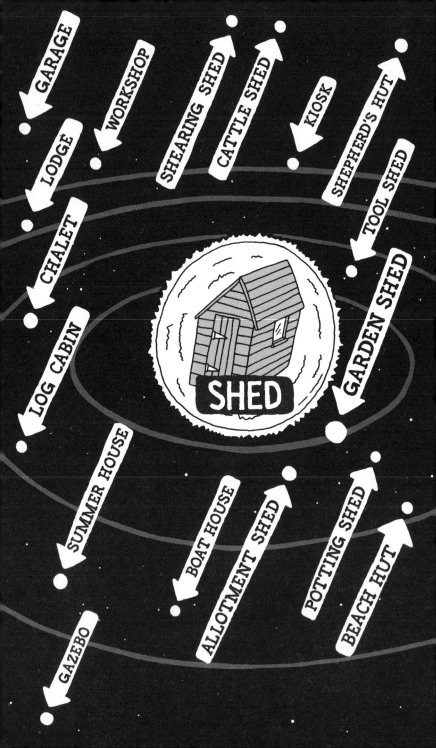

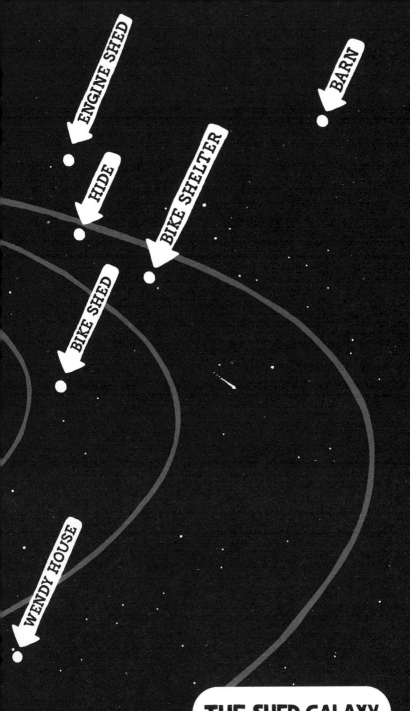

ENGINE SHED

BARN

HIDE

BIKE SHELTER

BIKE SHED

WENDY HOUSE

THE SHED GALAXY

Shed *History*

Very few sheds have had pivotal roles in world history. The Armistice that concluded World War I was signed in a railway carriage and not a shed. In the American Civil War, General Lee's surrender was taken at Appomattox Courthouse and not a shed. In the English Civil War, Charles II hid in an oak tree and not a shed. While mighty corporations, such as Hewlett-Packard, IKEA and Harley Davidson started life in a shed, few sheds have shaped the great moments of history, apart from the sheds at Bletchley Park.

Shed Origins

The word shed is rooted in England's agriculturally rich past. First recorded in 1481 as *shadde*, possibly a variant of shade, it was used to describe an open shelter. "A yearde in whiche was a shadde where in were six grete dogges," is a much-quoted phrase to describe the Cromagnon Man of sheds.

Up until Chaucer's time, French was the *lingua franca* of the Norman-dominated country and hence there are no references to sheds in the Domesday Book. With no universal spellings for centuries, the Old English word has cropped up in a variety of different forms, including shadde, shad and shedde. The Anglo Saxon word "shud", which means "a cover", may also have been a source for the universally loved structure. In 1440, a "shud" was defined as a "... schudde, hovel, swyne kote or howse of sympyl hyllynge to kepe yn beestys."

The Shed Tsar

Sheds may not have been pivotal in world affairs, but one bore witness to the last days of Tsar Nicholas II. Seen here after the Bolshevik revolution, in the garden at Alexander Palace, during the imperial family's internment at Tsarskoe Selo in 1917, is the last head of the Romanov empire (right of frame), spade in hand. Not digging. The Tsarina, or Czarina, is by the shed holding a parasol with her two daughters, the grand duchesses. Not digging either.

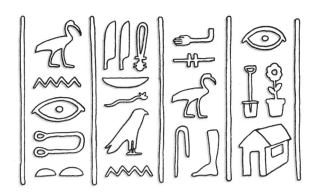

⟨image⟩ Shed The God

Sometimes when you read Wikipedia you think they might be having a laugh. There is an entry that places 'Shed' back in ancient Egyptian times. Has it been placed there by the same kind of people who spotted a kebab in the Bayeux Tapestry and are probably trying to assert a reference to a branch of Phones4u in the Domesday Book? Who knows. For the record, this is what someone scratched on an ancient bit of papyrus (that was probably found in the back of a Dead Sea shed).

> 'Shed is an Ancient Egyptian deity, popularly called, "the saviour" and is first recorded after the Amarna Period. Representing the concept of salvation he is identified with Horus and in particular Horus the Child. Rather than have formal worship in a temple or as an official cult, he appears to have been a god that ordinary Egyptians looked to save them from illness, misfortune or danger. Shed has been viewed as a form of helper for those in need when state authority or the King's help is found wanting. The increased reliance on divine assistance could even extend to saving a person from the underworld, even to providing a substitute, and lengthening a person's time in this world.'

So there you have it – Shed is an ancient deity who can be worshipped. What a pity we've just missed the 2011 census. There's always that question about religion where everyone likes to have a laugh and say they're a confirmed Jedi. Now we have an alternative answer...

Ernest's Boat Shed

Ernest Shackleton's ill-fated Trans-Antarctic expedition of 1914–16 was a triumph born out of failure. That triumph was only made possible by a bit of improvised shed building on Elephant Island.

The Anglo-Irish explorer set out in his ship *Endurance* in 1914 on a mission to cross the great antarctic continent by dog sled, but before the ship could even deliver the explorers to their drop-off point it was gripped by unseasonally early ice. The trip then became a battle of survival as the *Endurance*, entombed in the ice floe, drifted helplessly with the ice pack and was eventually crushed by the pressure of ice. On 9 April, 1916, the ice floe that the crew had decamped to broke in half and Shackleton ordered his men into the three lifeboats to head for the nearest land. After five days at sea, the exhausted men landed their three lifeboats at the remote Elephant Island, the first time they had stood on solid ground for 497 days.

Far from any shipping route, and unlikely to be found, Shackleton ordered that two of the lifeboats be made into one large wooden hut while he and a crew of five set off for the Norwegian whaling station on South Georgia, 800 miles away. If Shackleton's journey across the storm-lashed Southern Ocean in an open boat, with only primitive navigation equipment, is not heroic enough, he and two men then had to traverse South Georgia's mountains and glaciers using only a carpenter's axe and 50 feet of rope.

After raising the alarm at Stromness his men were finally picked up in August 1916. Thanks to Shackleton's extraordinary courage and leadership, and the improvised wooden hut on Elephant Island, he didn't lose a single man from the *Endurance* crew.

SHED FACT

Pink Floyd star David Gilmour had to pull down a bright yellow shed in the back yard of his listed £3 million seafront mansion or face prosecution in 2011. East Sussex Council had to act when a NIMBY neighbour objected to his modest (but garish) bicycle store.

Ernest Shackleton and his *Endurance* crew set off on the 800-mile trip in the *James Caird* lifeboat, named after one of the expedition's sponsors. The other two lifeboats, the *Dudley Docker* and the *Stanhope-Whitcomb*, were turned over and used as a shelter for the remaining 22 men for the four months that followed.

The Colossus Mark II (bombe)
computer at Bletchley Park, 1943.
Notice that this important wartime
work has been entrusted to a hut
and not a building.

◢ The Sheds That Shortened World War II

They were the wooden huts that shortened the war by two years. The decryption of enemy signals that took place at Bletchley Park was pivotal in the Allied victory. Winston Churchill referred to the Bletchley staff as, "The geese that laid the golden eggs and never cackled."

At the beginning of the war the Government Code and Cypher School moved into the mansion at Bletchley Park, but such was the volume of work generated that soon the mansion and its stables and cottages were overflowing. Huts had to be built.

Bletchley's wooden huts contained translation staff, cryptographers and the Tommy Flowers-devised primitive computer or "bombe", housed in Hut 11, that cracked the German Tunny enciphering codes.

Such was the success of the Bletchley Park intelligence material, code-named "Ultra", that on the eve of D-Day, the whereabouts of all but two of Rommel's 58 divisions in France were known.

After the war many of the huts fell into dilapidation, while the staff refused to talk about their roles and the full significance of the work at Bletchley was unknown. Today, there is a Bletchley museum that honours the work of Alan Turing, Bill Tutte and Tommy Flowers and the many hundreds of support workers who helped save lives and shorten the war.

Do not talk at meals ...
Do not talk in the transport ...
Do not talk travelling ...
Do not talk in the billet ...
Do not talk by your own fireside ...
Be careful even in your Hut...

(Warning notice to staff at Bletchley Park issued in 1942.)

Hidden in a *Shed*

Sheds are ideal places to stash things away that shouldn't be in the main house. This can be anything from firearms to pornography, or things that men just can't bear to throw away, "because it might come in useful some day…" Over a lifetime it can become an enormous haul. The fact that sheds soon become infested with spiders and the occasional scuttling mouse, and take on a distinctively shed-like smell, doesn't make them conducive to female rummaging and the kind of critical scrutiny that would have these items evicted in seconds from the domestic abode.

Woke Up This Morning – And Got Myself A Gun...

It was a bit like the episode of *The Sopranos* where mafia boss Tony goes and hides his guns at his elderly mother's nursing home. American police arrested John Orlowski after finding him in a shed with $20,000 and a MAC-10 assault weapon. He was apprehended while breaking into a shed at his estranged wife's home after she reported him lurking round the backyard, which contravened a restraining order.

The previous month, Orlowski, from Massachusetts, had been ordered to hand over his entire gun collection: 121 firearms, including handguns, rifles, shotguns and an Uzi submachine gun, that had been stuffed carelessly into plastic boxes around his home.

He allegedly told police later that he'd hidden a .357 handgun in his parents' slow cooker.

Going, Going, Gone

A local auctioneer triggered a full-scale police alert when he discovered a hand grenade stored in a West Midlands shed. Charles Hanson, of Hanson's Auctioneers in Lichfield, was sorting material into lots for a house clearance sale. While going through the contents of a shed belonging to 94-year-old Mary Craddock of Lichfield Road, Brownhills, he found the grenade – thought to date back to World War II. Police took it away for the last, the very last and final time after Mr. Hanson indicated he wouldn't be putting it under the hammer.

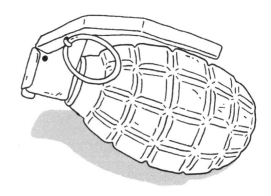

Raising The Roof

A Cheltenham man was on the point of demolishing an old shed in his garden when he decided to make one last search to check that it was completely empty. Paul Fittock discovered a World War II hand grenade on a shelf in the wooden rafters minutes before he was due to attack it with a sledgehammer. RAF bomb disposal officers placed the device in a metal box and took it to a quarry to be detonated.

Found In A Shed: One Childhood

Men can be secretive creatures. For decades, Aberystwyth housewife Brenda Rowlands wondered what her husband Dewi kept under lock and key in the wooden chest he stored in his shed. When asked, he had always "politely refused to say". After he passed away at the age of 77, Mrs. Rowlands got to find out. Inside was her husband's collection of his childhood; a wonderful array of pre World War II games, wooden toys and animals.

Mrs. Rowlands told the *Daily Telegraph*, "Inside was a clockwork train set, clockwork helicopter, soldiers made of lead and wooden farm and zoo animals all from the 1920s and 30s. It was amazing. There were home-made farm buildings, a wooden alphabet, and games of snakes and ladders and ludo. I also found a small tin containing marbles, broken toys, nuts and bolts, just the things which might have been found in the pockets of a small boy during the 1930s."

Mrs. Rowlands, 70, said, "Years ago I remember asking him about what was in it and him saying to me 'just leave it' and I never questioned him again."

A Shedload Of Cash – £29m Actually

Two Japanese sisters were accused of masterminding the biggest case of inheritance tax evasion Japan has seen – by hiding the cash in a shed.

Japanese inland revenue officials believe Hatsue Shimizu, 64, and Yoshiko Ishii, 55, stashed away notes to the value of £29 million, a fortune inherited from their businessman father after his death in 2004.

The tax officials said the women had registered only a tiny fraction of their inheritance to avoid taxes on the rest. Their windfall was allegedly discovered in boxes and paper bags in a shed next to their house in Osaka.

She'll Be Right

The life's work of one of Australia's most important anthropologists was discovered in the shed of a New South Wales cattleman.

The groundbreaking works of Caroline Tennant-Kelly, close friend of the famed American anthropologist Margaret Mead, were thought to have been destroyed until they came to light in Graham Gooding's cattle shed. He had kept the papers, documents and research records, some stretching back to the 1930s, "because it looked like the works of an exceptional person… I thought that if I took care of it, someday someone would appear looking for it," Mr. Gooding said. And the University of Queensland did.

Relax in a shed

SHED FACT

25% of men say their shed is the only place they can relax and unwind in.

No Gnome To Go To

A woman living in St. Germain-du-Corbéis near Alençon in Normandy found 100 garden gnomes stashed away in the shed of a property she acquired. Further investigation revealed that the house had been used as the HQ for the *Front de Liberation des Nains de Jardin* (Garden Gnome Liberation Front). In 1996 they set out to liberate the garden gnomes of northern France and set them free in the forest. They only curtailed their activities when homeowners started to press charges for theft. After the haul was uncovered, French police said no one had come forward to claim any of them.

SHED FACT

47% of men say they've spent a whole day in their shed at a time.

Not So Cool For Cats

A woman in Pasadena, California, was facing prosecution after 140 cats were found in a shed in her backyard. The woman, known as "Tammy" and described by a California blogging site as "bat shit insane", was investigated by America's equivalent of the RSPCA, the Humane Society. Twenty volunteers from the Pasadena branch arrived to remove the animals.

"I have never seen one single cat in the whole two years she's lived here," one neighbour told the *San Gabriel Valley Tribune*. "When she moved here two years ago she told us she had only 10 cats, but she came late at night so no one would know," said Wilfred Duran, another neighbour.

The Radioactive Boy Scout

The first thing that Dottie Pease knew about David Hahn's attempt to build a model breeder nuclear reactor in his shed was when three men in white suits and respirators crossed her lawn holding Geiger counters, en route for her neighbour's backyard. It was like a scene from *The X-Files*. The men, who were from the U.S. Environmental Protection Agency, broke the shed up, filled 39 barrels and sent it off to a low-level waste disposal site in the Great Salt Lake Desert.

Hahn's attempt to produce cheap energy at the bottom of his garden had resulted in dangerous levels of radiation at his Michigan home in 1995. The 17-year-old Eagle Scout, who got his scouting merit badge for atomic energy in 1991, realised that he might have got too much radioactive material in one place when he started picking up signals on his home Geiger counter, five houses away from his shed. But by placing some of the material in the trunk of his old Pontiac to split the sources up, he made discovery of his project more likely. When police pulled him over on a separate incident, they found what they thought was a home-made atomic bomb in the back.

Hahn told author Ken Silverstein how he meticulously collected

and refined beryllium, americium from smoke detectors, radium from luminous paint, thorium from gas mantles and lithium from batteries. Of his exposure to radioactivity, he said, "I don't believe I took more than five years off my life."

SHED FACT

Where would you expect a specialist in media law to operate from? LA, New York, London? Barrister Peter Smith's claim to fame is that he runs the only media law practice out of a wooden shed in the small Highlands village of Strathpeffer. Face to face meetings clearly aren't his speciality.

The Sheds Of Hazard

Whereas Britain has to make do with finding single World War II hand grenades in sheds, they can always go bigger and better in the USA. In 2011 the Renville County Sheriff's Department, in rural Minnesota, found 100 sticks of dynamite in a shed. A disused farm outbuilding near Hector was found to have a 40-year-old stock of the explosives, which someone had left there in a container.

"Years ago, dynamite was commonly used to remove rocks, trees, beaver dams and other structures in rural areas," reported Renville County Sheriff, Scott Hable, "but over time, it becomes unstable and specially trained professionals are required to move and destroy it."

A chip off the old blockhead

SHED FACT

Comedy star Oliver Hardy was just as good at DIY in real life as he was on screen. Together with the brother of his wife Lucille, he set about making some large chicken coops in a shed in their backyard. In true Laurel and Hardy fashion, when the pair of blockheads came to take them outside they realised they were too big to fit through the shed door and they all had to be taken apart again and reconstructed outside.

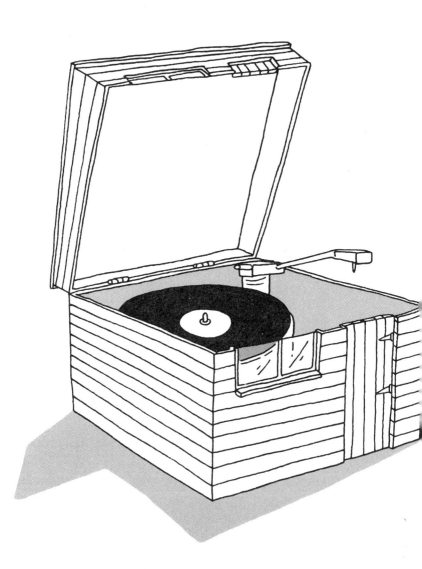

Sheds in *Music*

What is the similarity between a post-punk Swindon band and the Norwegian composer who wrote *In The Hall of the Mountain King*? It's a shed. While Edvard Grieg's sat alongside a tranquil Norwegian lake, former XTC frontman Andy Partridge's favourite music room is at the bottom of the garden of his Wiltshire home. Thanks to a combination of stage fright and tinnitus, one of the most intelligent writers in rock music doesn't go out on the road any more. Instead he devotes himself to writing, recording and producing other artists on his Fuzzy Warbles record label from his shed. Who needs Abbey Road...

◼—— XTC

West country band XTC shot to public prominence in the post-punk era with songs such as *Making Plans For Nigel* and *Generals and Majors*. Lead singer and self-confessed big mouth Andy Partridge was their guiding light along with songwriter Colin Moulding.

Around 1990, with his attic groaning under the weight of recording equipment, Andy moved the recording gear out to his shed. And he's been there ever since. XTC have made it clear they will not be touring any time soon – if ever again – and so Partridge constantly uses his shed to make demos for songs to take into the studio, write songs with the likes of Cathy Dennis or Terry Hall or to record other artists.

Among the first things recorded in the shed were demos for the Gus Dudgeon-produced *Nonsuch* album which included the classic single *The Ballad of Peter Pumpkinhead*. After it was released people jumped to the conclusion that the song was a fable about JFK, Lennon or Jesus.

"A lot of people have theories about what the song's about," says Andy. "Actually the name's from a Halloween lantern I carved. I stuck it on a fence post in my garden and every day I'd go past it on the way to my shed. And every day it would decay a bit more. I felt so sorry for it, I thought I'd make it a hero in a song..."

Robyn Hitchcock

U.S. *Billboard* magazine reported in 2008 that former Soft Boy Robyn Hitchcock and Andy Partridge were working on a collaborative album together. "It's a self-generating project," Hitchcock told the music title. "I write the words on the train going up to Swindon and then, bang, we record it in his shed."

Shed Zeppelin? No Shed Seven

Formed in 1990 these Brit pop exponents from York didn't get their name from the garden variety. They had formed a band and were looking for a name. On a return trip to York, as they approached York railway station, they noticed a small shed on the sidings with the sign 'Shed 7'.

Greatest Album Ever Recorded In A Shed

Sunshine Hit Me – the Mercury Music prize-nominated debut album by The Bees is one of the finest examples of an album recorded in a shed. It includes the hit A *Minha Menina*. It was recorded in Paul Butler's dad's shed in the Isle of Wight.

Chris Difford from Squeeze talking about his allotment shed, Rhubarb House, in Rye

"Here in my sanctuary I find the serenity I always seem to need, here I can look at the world from the inside out. I can smell the fertilizers of my youth and touch the hanging fruits of tomorrow as they ripen on the vine. Here I can think about my life. It's a good place to be, it's my cloud nine. Welcome."

◀━━ *Man In A Shed* – By Nick Drake

The greatest song ever written about a shed is *Man in a Shed* by tragic singer-songwriter Nick Drake. It first appeared on the album *Five Leaves Left*, released in September 1969. Drake was an introverted genius with a chronic fear of performing live. The lyrics for *Man in a Shed* can be interpreted many different ways, but music critics are united in the belief that it is not about shed maintenance.

> Well there was a man who lived in a shed
> Spent most of the days out of his head
> For his shed was rotten, let in the rain
> Said it was enough to drive any man insane.
>
> So leave your house come into my shed
> Please stop my world from raining through my head
> Please don't think I'm not your sort
> You'll find that sheds are nicer than you thought.

Thomas Dolby's Shed

1980s electronic popster Thomas *Hyperactive* Dolby now lives on the west coast of America, but doesn't regret a move from a bricks and mortar studio to his shed. "I invested in a small studio in West London, filled it full of the latest equipment and in the five years I had it I didn't write a decent bit of music. So it's no great surprise that I ended up here in this garden shed. It's got everything I need, and no guilt attached. It never needs heating as the equipment takes care of that. It glows at night and looks pretty high-tech, in a ham radio operator sort of way, but when my roadies clear it out for a gig, it returns to its humble beginnings and you're almost tempted to wheel a lawnmower in there.

"One time I was working late and a little note was slipped under the door, written in crayon by my then seven-year-old son: 'Dear Daddy. I hope yue ar having a good time in yor shed. Love Graham.' I still have it pinned to the door frame."

The enigmatic Nick Drake,
actually in a shed for the cover of his
album, *Five Leaves Left*. It's unknown
whether the follow-up album was going
to be called *And A Couple of Spiders*.

Slade's Screen Shed

Brummy glam rockers Slade appear with pigeons and pigeon shed (all right, loft) to show their working class roots in their debut feature film, *Flame*. The movie, which spawned the album *Slade in Flame*, cast them as a fictional band Iron Rod who are discovered playing on the UK pub circuit. Noddy Holder, Jim Lea, Dave Hill and Don Powell play boys from the Black Country manipulated by unscrupulous managers etc. on their not-so-glittering path to the top. The days of bands making films, e.g. Beatles, David Essex, are long gone. Imagine the Coldplay film...? Well, it certainly wouldn't feature a shed.

Disco Shed

One of the stars of the Latitude Festival since 2009 has been the Disco Shed. The Disco Shed started life in 2006 as a humble 8 x 6 foot garden shed which was then mounted on a trailer and stuffed with a giant sound system. Promoters Peepshow Paddy and Aidan 'Count' Skylarkin take the disco shed, complete with the odd gnome and garden implement, around the festival circuit every summer. They've even started taking it indoors in winter. In fact it's been so successful that they have their own Disco Shed merchandise and have moved on to Shed Mark II with individual toolsheds to hold the cabinets. It's what every garden party needs.

Snoop Dogg's Shed

Just like Swindon's finest, LA rap star Snoop Dogg has written hit records in his shed. The West Coast rapper decided that he wanted a bigger backyard retreat in 2008 and decided to auction the Snoop outhouse where he'd written hits such as *Drop It Like It's Hot*. With bids starting at $1000 the money raised went to his project – Snoop's Youth Football League.

"I've had this shed since the turn of the century. I've beaten over 1,000 people on Madden in it, watched football game tapes, seen the Lakers win championships, and most of all, written hits in it."

No bling was included but Snoop signed the building before it was collected by its new owner. "Enjoy it. And let the legend live on, ya dig?!"

"The shed is pretty minute. It's 12 feet by 8 feet and stuffed with equipment. You don't have room to swing a Strat."

Andy Partridge

◗━━ A Very Irregular Shed

Syd Barrett, founder member of Pink Floyd, and inspiration for the Floyd track *Shine On You Crazy Diamond* was a keen cyclist and gardener. After his death in 2006 his family put his house and some of the contents up for sale through local auctioneers Cheffins. In 2009 the Barrett shed, in which he'd written neither of the first Floyd singles – *Arnold Layne* and *See Emily Play* – was put up for auction on eBay.

It was described, thus: "This shed is from the garden of the house Syd Barrett spent the last 30-odd years of his life living in. It has been painted oxblood and cream inside by Syd and contains furniture he built and painted himself; a press with two opening doors, a hose reel, a shelf and several other adaptations, the most curious of which is a device for retrieving his house keys even when he had also misplaced the key of the shed.

"The door of the shed seems also to have been made or at least fitted by Syd, and it is painted green with the hinges picked out in a chalk blue colour (a style favoured by Syd). Some planks have been replaced with fence shiplap at the far end."

The starting price was £1000. It didn't sell.

SHED FACT

Sheds are good for relationships, it's official. Whilst over a third of men feel a shed improves their relationship, their partners also agree – 20% of women see a shed as a positive influence on their man.

Radioshed

In early 1996, Radiohead started rehearsing and recording *OK Computer* in the Canned Applause studio, a converted shed near Didcot, Oxfordshire.

Songs From The Shed

Jon Earl won the prestigious Shed of the Year 2011 prize, organised by the groundbreaking Shedblog.co.uk website.

Jon started his Songs from the Shed project in 2009 – turning his 12 x 10 foot outbuilding in Clevedon, Somerset into a space where he records music performances from local bands and any passing international acts who care to drop in.

Jon inherited many of the decorative artefacts (including oars and a trombone) in the shed from the previous owner and originally intended to launch a Cheese and Cider Society and use his shed as HQ. But after a conversation down the pub, the plan got changed – as plans down the pub usually do.

Jon records the sessions on a Canon video camera, edits them and then uploads them to his website – www.songsfromtheshed.com.

Fairport Convention, Steve Harley, shed-loving Chris Difford and even the 20-strong Gasworks Choir have popped into the award-winning shed, and after all the publicity in 2011 the number of acts wanting to get into Jon's shed has increased.

In The Hut Of The Mountain King

There's quiet and there's very quiet. Norwegian pianist and composer Edvard Grieg (*Peer Gynt*) needed absolute quiet to compose his music and so he built himself a shed down by the lake to get the kind of concert hall quiet that he appreciated. In his house at Troldhaugen the noise from the kitchen or constant visitors interrupted his work and so from 1891 he was able to retreat to his lakeside hut.

Even there he wasn't immune from distraction, though. An unfamiliar sound or a boat rowing on the lake was enough to stop him mid-quaver.

After he left his shed at the end of the day he would leave a note to any would-be Norwegian burglar: "If anyone should break in here, please leave the musical scores, since they have no value to anyone except Edvard Grieg." Which is clearly the forerunner to white van man's: "No tools left in this van overnight."

A Really Sound Shed

Vince Clarke, formerly of Depeche Mode and Yazoo, and Martin Ware, formerly of Human League and Heaven 17, were asked by the V&A Museum to decorate a garden shed as part of their 2004 *The Other Flower Show* exhibition.

The electronic music pioneers had rebranded themselves as artists creating 3D soundscapes. Their shed was badged as "Town and Country" and was described as "comprising a variety of low-level 3D immersive sound recordings of British countryside locations. They transported the visitor to forests, moorland, cliff tops and lakesides purely through the emotive and atmospheric intensity of sound. At intervals a cacophony of urban noise and lights jolted unsuspecting visitors from their reverie."

(Read more about other pieces in the exhibition in Shed Art p.50)

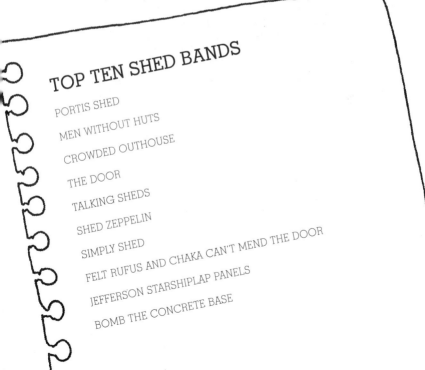

TOP TEN SHED BANDS

PORTIS SHED

MEN WITHOUT HUTS

CROWDED OUTHOUSE

THE DOOR

TALKING SHEDS

SHED ZEPPELIN

SIMPLY SHED

FELT RUFUS AND CHAKA CAN'T MEND THE DOOR

JEFFERSON STARSHIPLAP PANELS

BOMB THE CONCRETE BASE

Created in a *Shed*

The shed stereotype that prevails over all others is that of the shed inventor, the eccentric genius who disappears into his shed and comes out with a highly efficient electric motor made from soup tins, or a wind-up clockwork radio. Items which, as it happens, were both devised in sheds. Wacky inventions aren't the only things of great worth created in sheds. Some of the world's most prestigious companies started life in small wooden premises before their idea caught fire. A shed can provide the extra space needed when the bedroom business becomes ripe for expansion, and it can provide the thinking space, free from the clutter and interruption of everyday life.

The Most Famous Chippie In The World

Forget pizzas, the world's greatest chippie was started in a hut. Harry Ramsden first started serving customers in 1928 from a wooden hut in White Cross, Guiseley near Leeds in Yorkshire. Three years later he moved into his "fish and chip palace" a swanky restaurant complete with fitted carpets, oak panelled walls and grand chandeliers. However, the original hut still stands on its original site adjacent to the main restaurant.

Its founder passed away in 1963 but Harry will be pleased to know that his restaurant holds the Guinness World Record for being the largest fish and chip shop in the world, serving nearly a million customers a year.

No Instant Success

Momofuku Ando was born in Taiwan in 1910 when it was part of the Japanese empire. Proving that it's never too late to start a shed-based business Ando invented the pot noodle in his shed at the age of 61. He lived to the ripe old age of 96 and was said to eat Chikin Ramen (chicken noodles) almost every day. Without his invention, millions of students and night-time security personnel across the world would go hungry every day and night. And there would be no Momofuku Ando Instant Ramen Museum either.

> Eventually, successful technology leads to huge corporations, research laboratories and great sprawling factories employing thousands of people between them. But the moment of inspiration is invariably a lonely experience in a shed of some sort.
>
> *James May's Magnificent Machines: How Men in Sheds Have Changed Our Lives*

More Soup Cans, Gromit

Cedric Lynch is probably the stereotypical shed inventor as envisioned by James May. Since the 1970s Cedric has been tucked away in his shed in Potters Bar perfecting a more efficient electric motor and even appeared on *Tomorrow's World* touting his designs. Engines are generally not very efficient things and while a steam engine is about 8% efficient, a diesel engine 40% efficient and electric engines about 75%, Cedric has managed to achieve a 93% efficiency rating with his invention.

Cedric's prototypes were made (in the grand Wallace and Gromit fashion) using flattened soup cans. Four of the engines he invented were installed in a boat that broke the World Speed Record for electrically driven vessels, at around 50mph.

Cedric is now working for the Agni Company producing electric motors in India. Reassuringly his Agni address in India is: Shed 37/38.

Black Jack's Shed

Australia's first F1 World Champion, Jack Brabham, started building his own racing cars in a shed in Esher, in Surrey. At the time he was under contract to the Cooper Car Company and though he owned a small petrol station and garage in nearby Chessington, he didn't want Cooper to find out what he was up to. And so the Brabham team, that would eventually be owned by Bernie Ecclestone and win World Championships with Nelson Piquet, started life in a secret shed.

An Appeal to Men in Sheds

In 2006, Defence Procurement minister Lord Drayson appealed directly to men in sheds to create a new intelligence gathering…wotsit. No small task this, the noble Lord wanted a device to scan ahead of patrolling soldiers to alert them to dangers in a complex and cluttered urban environment.

"So we are looking for scientists and engineers to use their brainpower to think about how they can come up with something to help our soldiers sort of see ahead, give them eyes in the back of their head," he explained.

The winning inventor would get a development contract from the MoD and the R.J. Mitchell Trophy, named after the man who designed the Spitfire.

Lord Drayson said: "If you go back through history there are lots of examples where really groundbreaking innovations have come out of garages and people working in their garden sheds."

Nobel Prize-Winning Shed Research

Marie Curie (1867–1934) is likely to remain the only two-time winner of the Nobel Prize who carried out the majority of their scientific work in a shed. The Polish-French Nobel laureate was awarded prizes in both physics and chemistry for her pioneering work in radiation – experiments that would lead to her premature death at 67. With little known about the damaging effects of radiation she would carry radioactive isotopes around in pockets and aprons and would store them liberally about her shed. Because of their proximity to such massive doses of radiation, important papers she wrote from the 1890s are deemed too dangerous to handle and along with a radioactive cookbook are stored in a lead-lined box.

Silicon Shed

Technology giant Hewlett-Packard or HP – if you want to confuse it with a brand of well-known sauce – is one of the many companies that started from shedlike premises. Though technically a garage, the structure at 367 Addison Avenue, Palo Alto, was detached from the main building and was to all intents and purposes a shed. Inside, Stanford University classmates Bill Hewlett and Dave Packard produced their fledgling company's first product – an audio oscillator – an electronic test instrument used by sound engineers.

It has since been refurbished and rebuilt and stands today as California Historic Landmark No. 976 "Birthplace of Silicon Valley".

Vorsprung Shed Teknik

Little did Gottlieb Daimler know that while he was toiling away on the world's first lightweight four-stroke internal combustion engine – in an extension to his greenhouse – Karl and Berthe Benz were doing the same in their shed. He and fellow inventor Wilhelm Maybach widened the garden path that led to the makeshift workshop at the bottom of the garden so that vehicles could be wheeled down to it. Their work was carried out in such secrecy in this remote garden building – servants were not allowed inside – that he was reported to the police for installing an illegal mint.

Which is what you need these days to afford a Mercedes Maybach. It's not known whether Otto Diesel had a shed, and no-one cares if former Nazi Felix Wankel did (he invented the rotary engine).

SHED FACT

1 in 5 people use their shed for an activity other than garden storage.

Made In Sweden

Ingvar Kamprad established IKEA in 1943 at the age of
17 in a shed two metres square. The company name is
a combination of his initials (Ingvar Kamprad) and
the first letters of the farm and village he grew up in
(Elmtaryd and Agunnaryd). When the fledgling business
got underway, flatpack furniture was not on the agenda,
Kamprad sold pens, matches, cigarette lighters, nylon
stockings and other disposable items in bulk.

In 1945 he moved into the mail order business and
finally in 1947 he took to selling his first furniture
products. By 1951 he had become so successful at
selling furniture he concentrated on that alone,
publishing the first IKEA catalogue that year. A shop
in Almhult followed in 1953, a showroom in 1958 and
the first overseas branch – Norway – in 1963.

Today it is one of the world's biggest private
companies employing over 127,000 people, giving
away free pencils and selling 24 billion euros' worth
of furniture, cutlery and candles. But no sheds.

Good Idea Mr. Ferodo

Boot salesman Herbert Frood was an observant sort. Travelling through the Peak District of Derbyshire he noticed how farmers and carters would attach leather boots to their wooden cart brakes to help them get down steep hills. The leather of the boot would give a much better grip against the metal rim of the wheel. Inspired, he set to work in his shed to produce brake shoes and by 1897 had hit on a compound of laminated hair and bitumen. He borrowed the letter 'E' from his wife Elizabeth, added it to his surname and formed Ferodo.

Herbert's brake shoes were a big success, taken up by the London General Omnibus Company and used in a variety of vehicles, including World War I tanks. The factory at Chapel Le Frith in Derbyshire soon expanded and is still in operation today with Herbert's pioneering shed preserved on the works bowling green.

F1 Shed

Ken Tyrrell started off his Formula 1 team in a woodshed – although technically speaking it was a fairly large woodshed as his family were timber merchants. Tyrrell went on to provide a World Championship winning car for Jackie Stewart and create the fabulous six-wheeled Tyrrell P34. They also provided a car for current F1 commentator Martin Brundle.

American Golf In A Shed

Cheshire businessman Howard Bilton earned himself £21m when he sold off his American Golf Discount chain in 2004. The retail giant of UK golfing started life in a shed bought for £36. Howard left school at 16 and after qualifying for his PGA badge got a job as golf professional at the Ashton-in-Makerfield course. There was no shop on the course and so he and brother Robert bought a shed, some stock and started trading.

The World's Smallest Production Line

William Harley met Arthur Davidson when they were both working for a metal fabrication company in Milwaukee; William was a draftsman and Arthur was a pattern maker, and in 1901 they set about making a motorcycle after their plans to build an outboard motor for fishing trips fell through. From a humble, 10 x 15 foot wooden shed emerged what would become the world's most charismatic motorcycle marque. With the help of Arthur's two brothers, William and Walter, three machines were produced in 1903 and again in 1904, until in 1906 they bought a site in Chester Street, Milwaukee (later to be renamed Juneau Avenue) and built their first factory.

Wind-Up Merchant

The doyen of the shed inventing world is Trevor Baylis OBE. The former stuntman turned inventor was frustrated that AIDS was spreading across Africa for the simple lack of health education and an absence of radios to spread the word. Then Baylis had his eureka moment. "I imagined someone listening close to the horn of an old gramophone. It was so obvious: if a clockwork gramophone could produce that sound, why not apply the idea to a radio?" Trev went straight to his shed-come-workshop and knocked out a prototype. After running up against typical British apathy towards new inventions his breakthrough came when he got to show his wind-up radio on BBC's *Tomorrow's World*.

Having cleared a lot more hurdles he eventually produced a radio that would play for an hour with only 20 seconds of winding and his philanthropic invention made it to Africa.

That Won't Workmate

You'd have thought that being Director of Engineering for Lotus racing cars would have been enough to keep him occupied, but no, Ron Hickman had an invention he wanted to bring to the world's attention.

One weekend in 1961 he was making a wardrobe at home and needed a support for the wood. So he put it on a chair… and ended up sawing through the wood and the chair. Thus the idea of what would become the Black & Decker Workmate was born. Initially Black & Decker rejected it and Stanley tools said that sales of the item would be in dozens, not hundreds.

So Ron started making them in his garden shed and they proved so popular that Black & Decker decided maybe they would license it after all. It's now sold in excess of 30 million.

> ## SHED FACT
>
> English Heritage say there are at least 52 Grade II listed sheds in England and Wales.

Shed *Art*

Sheds can be many things in art. They can be the blank canvas on which an artist displays his or her oeuvre. They can be the studio in which they create great masterpieces. Or they can become the *object d'art* themselves, at which point they are transformed from a workaday 'shed' and, using artspeak, become a 'piece' or an 'installation'. Tracey Emin's beach hut was minding its own business in Whitstable when it was suddenly elevated to the stature of installation, while a shed in a Swiss field couldn't quite believe it when it won the Turner Prize (along with the rest of the nation's art sceptics).

Tracey's Hut R.I.P.

Emin used the space in her Whitstable hut to make various naked self-portraits. When it was destroyed in the Momart fire she was upset. She had related to the single room as a powerfully eroticised space with associations far beyond the aesthetic.

"It had stood in Whitstable for 25 years before I had it," she says of the blue shack that she bought with friend Sarah Lucas and shared with her boyfriend of the time, Carl Freedman. "It travelled to America and back again. It had a life. Like the tent. It had real spirit. I never imagined them not being in the world."

Tracey Emin's Beach Hut

Tracey Emin bought herself a Whitstable beach hut in 1992. She used the hut as a weekend retreat and really enjoyed the idea of owning a place of her own that wasn't a tent: "I was completely broke and it was brilliant, having your own property by the sea."

She spent time there with soon-to-be gallery owner Carl Freedman and removed it in 1999 when it suddenly became an 'installation' with the title, *The Last Thing I Said to You is Don't Leave Me Here*. She also used it as the backdrop to various self-portraits reminiscent of the Austrian artist Egon Schiele; but more shed-based.

Sadly it was destroyed in the 2005 Momart warehouse fire that also claimed great works by the Chapman Brothers and Damien Hirst. Similar Whitstable beach installations can be hired though whitstablebeachhut.co.uk

Negative Shed

Rachel Whiteread is a sculptor who is most famous for producing casts of spaces within objects – negative spaces. She won the Turner Prize in 1993 for her cast of the inside of a Victorian House, 193 Grove Road in East London, which was then knocked down to reveal the work of art. (It was going to be demolished anyway). Which was subsequently knocked down by Tower Hamlets in 1994. As a follow-up she produced *Negative Shed*, the cast of an inside of a shed.

THE SHED AS CANVAS

In 2004, the Victoria and Albert Museum decided to challenge the Chelsea Flower Show by putting on *The Other Flower Show: Artists' Garden Sheds*. They, "brought together a group of contemporary artists and designers to explore the formal qualities of flowers, gardens and nature. Each was invited to transform a garden shed into a creative and conceptual alternative to the traditional flower show."

Displayed in the V&A garden, each shed functioned as a blank canvas on which the individual artist could express themselves. Promotional material for the event put it into context: "There is something quintessentially English about a garden shed. It implies far more than simple garden storage: shelter at a rainy garden party, an enthusiast's workshop, a place for retreat, or perhaps for something more untoward."

VISUAL ARTIST HEATHER BARNETT STUCK SEEDS ON THE WALL OF HER SHED AND PHOTOGRAPHED THEM GROWING.

"*Rooted in Time and Motion paid homage to great moments of scientific inspiration and in particular the work of Sir Isaac Newton. On a scientific level, it examined the notion of gravity, time and motion, from the growth of a single mustard seed to the planetary movement in our solar system.*"

TORD BOONTJE'S WORK WAS DESCRIBED AS HOVERING BETWEEN DESIGN, CRAFT AND VISUAL ART. HE PUT HIS SHED ON STILTS AND MADE IT INTO A CHILDREN'S DEN.

"*His current body of work Wednesday is an evolving collection of chairs, tables, glass, lights and other objects; mixing the handmade and machine-made; the historical and digital. His work has evolved from an interest in decoration, homeliness and novelty.*"

So, a bit like IKEA, really.

CHRIS TAYLOR AND CRAIG WOOD PRODUCED A LOT OF BLANK WALLPAPER FOR PEOPLE TO FILL IN THEMSELVES. HAD THEY NOT BEEN PUKKA ARTISTS WITH VISION AND TITLES LIKE 'CURATOR' IN THEIR CVS THIS WOULD HAVE BEEN A LAZY-ARSED MASTERSTROKE:

"Their wallpapers focus on interaction. Using 'dot-to-dot', 'notation' and 'colouring-in' as their formats, they offer the viewer an opportunity to participate in the process and complete the design. The reductive nature of the designs have the familiar simplicity of a child's colouring book and hark back to the American Minimalist aesthetic. But the designs are just a starting point and the project is essentially about collaboration. The artists prescribe the strategy but the conclusion of the work relies on the creativity and involvement of the visitors."

TRACEY EMIN, ALWAYS EFFICIENT WITH HER USE OF STUFF, PUT THE PROPS SHE'D MADE FOR A JEAN COCTEAU STAGE PLAY IN HER SHED.

"Re-assembled, in her shed, they were carefully choreographed to symbolise desire, love, jealousy and hate, which have become trademark characteristics of Emin's work. Honesty, humour and poetry underpin Emin's unnervingly confessional oeuvre."

SCULPTOR ANTHONY GORMLEY WAS NOT OFFERED THE CHANCE TO FILL THE SHED WITH NAKED MODELS OF HIMSELF. PROBABLY DUE TO HEIGHT RESTRICTIONS.

✂ ShedBoatShed

The 2005 Turner Prize winner took Tracey Emin's and the V&A's artistic efforts with sheds one stage further. Simon Starling won the prestigious event with his *ShedBoatShed* installation. The story goes that Simon saw the shed on the banks of the Rhine (presumably bought it) converted it into a boat and floated it downstream seven miles – with all the bits he hadn't used bundled inside – and then reconstructed it as a shed in a Swiss museum.

According to the Tate Gallery's curator Rachel Tant, Starling is "interested in the creation of objects; he is a researcher, traveller, narrator. He looks at how things got to be the way they are, and reasserts a human connection between processes we take for granted."

As the building doesn't seem to have any natural curves to it, and doesn't look like the most watertight of structures, it probably should have been named *ShedRaftShed*. In response, the *Daily Mirror* made their own standard 8 x 6 foot apex shed into a boat and paddled it across Sefton Park Lake in Liverpool. Because they couldn't convert it back they called theirs, *ShedBoatBoat*. The Tate wasn't interested.

BoatShedStudio

French impressionist painter Claude Monet was very much like Ratty from *Tales of the Riverbank* – they both liked nothing better than messing about in boats. From December 1871 to 1878 he lived at Argenteuil, a village on the right bank of the river Seine near Paris, so he was able to spend a lot of time on the water.

Monet was an artist who preferred to sketch nature at first hand and he had a particular gift portraying the reflections and movement of water. So to aid his proximity to nature, Claude converted a boat into a floating studio by adding a shed-like structure, as can be seen in his work *Boat Studio*.

Artist Damien Hirst at The Wallace Collection, London, for an exhibition of his paintings in October, 2009. The collection comprised 25 new paintings all done in his Devon shed.

Something I Made In Me Shed

In 2009 Damien Hirst confessed to spending a lot of his time in his shed. The former *enfant terrible* of Brit art, whose shark in formaldehyde drew worldwide attention, told Radio 4's *Front Row* programme that he had retreated down the garden path to dabble in oils. "For two years... the paintings were embarrassing and I didn't want anyone to come in," he said of work produced in his studio shed in the garden of his Devon farmhouse.

"It felt awful for two years. I thought, 'if I die now, people are going to find these paintings and it's going to be horrible'."

SHED FACT

It is estimated that there are around 23,000 beach huts in the UK. Bournemouth alone has 1800.

 Shed: An Exploded View

Sheds may have been the subject of artist expression over the last few years, but it was Cornelia Parker who started off all this shed-flattening, shed moulding, shed rebuilding malarkey with her *Cold Dark Matter* exhibition. Back in 1991 she had taken all the unwanted things from her friends' garden sheds and stuffed them into a traditional shiplap panelled shed and erected it in the Chisenhale Gallery in London. After photographing it in place, it was taken away and given to the army who blew it up at the School of Ammunition near Banbury. Then all the pieces were carted back to the gallery and hung from the walls and ceilings from tiny threads. Around it was a constellation of burnt and damaged unloved objects, singed books, old ice skates, a bicycle wheel etc.

It gave a new meaning to the term exploded view.

Splashes Of Colour By The Seaside

A more practical example of shed art and shed beauty is the Dendy Street beach huts in Melbourne. Dendy Street Beach, just south of Middle Brighton, hosts a vestige of Victorian Australia. Back in 1862 they were located at the water's edge at the end of Bay Street, placed there in a bid to protect the modesty of lady bathers in their transition from promenader to bather. Over the passing years they were transformed into a practical beach store and when the tram line was completed from St Kilda to Brighton, the clamour for more 'bathing boxes' increased. Many more were built between 1908 and 1911 and as many as 200 may have existed before the Great Depression ruined everybody's fun.

Up until 2008 there were 82 of the beach huts painted in bold, colourful patterns which had become a tourist image of Melbourne. With selling prices at A$200,000 the local council planned to raise A$1 million by installing a further six.

Shed For The beach

Is it the inside of a shed, or is it a series of linked micro environments? Alun Ward's *Transporter Mix* installation / shed was a participatory piece shown at OVADA, an Oxford gallery, in 2009. And it was a bit of fun as well. Inside a shed he'd put a series of different outdoor surfaces, such as turf, shingle, sand, earth and woodland litter. The viewer entered the shed, having first taken off their shoes and socks and strapped on a pair of headphones. They were then played ambient sound recordings from the environments they were walking on: woodland, hillside, beaches, lawns and riversides. Participants were invited to close their eyes and see what the combination of sounds and feelings conjured up: "The combination of auditory and sensory input serves to transport the participant to remembered or imaginary locations."

If he'd ended the experience with shingle underfoot and the sounds of the beach with an ice cream van, they could have made a fortune from selling acacia and stem ginger Cornettos.

Shed identity

SHED FACT

Women are more likely to give fancy names to their sheds than men. If a garden shed is used for an activity other than storage, such as an office or for recreation, women will call it the 'studio', the 'office', the 'cabin' or the 'lodge' – whereas men are more likely to call it the shed.

Churchill, Can You Paint In Your Shed…?

Damien Hirst was following in the footsteps of many artists over the years who have created a studio space in a garden shed. When Winston Churchill felt the 'black dog' of depression tailing him, he would retreat to his shed in the garden of his country estate in Kent and paint his miseries away. After a few preliminary strokes on canvas he would often note that this wasn't the beginning of the end of the composition, but it was the end of the beginning. Ironically Adolf Hitler was also a keen artist but nobody took his art seriously.

SHED FACT

32% of men under 35 wish they had a shed
to call their own.

Sheds *in the News*

Sheds are often in the news for a whole host of different reasons. Unusual things come to light in them (usually a range of munitions), they get blown places in gale-force winds, or a megastar's hippy half brother is found living in one. They also take the blame for allegedly detaining missing pets. How often is the phrase, "Please check you sheds and outbuildings" seen on missing pet posters? As though for some reason sheds felt some ill will to pets wandering in and conspired to separate them from their loving owners. Usually it's another household feeding your perfidious puss, but in this chapter, we actually do have one shed bang to rights for their crime of pet hate.

Shed S.O.S.

The Sun labeled pipe-layer Stephen Lynch a DIY Disaster in 2007 after his plans to build a shed got hopelessly out of hand. Stephen, 41, from Coventry had intended to build a shed in his back garden, but then the plan changed. "I decided I wanted two big outbuildings rather than a little shed, so I bought an £18,500 mini digger to make it easier."

But instead of just digging out the footings, Stephen decided to go a little further and excavate 200 tons of earth to make basements for his outbuildings. When the massive hole got to 40ft by 30ft and 6.5 ft deep, and very close to neighbouring fences, there were fears it would undermine adjacent properties. A local housing association stepped in and won a court injunction to make him fill the crater in again. With lawyers and engineers' costs added to the bill for refilling the massive hole, the cost of making good was likely to add up to £50,000.

How many 8 x 10 foot apex sheds could you have bought for that?

> ## SHED FACT
>
> 23% of shed owners say they have slept or thought about sleeping in their shed.

Stopping The Shed Door From Banging...

New Malden pensioner Betty Johnson used an unexploded World War II shell as her shed doorstop for over a decade. She inherited the unusual shed accessory when she bought her house in Knightwood Crescent in the late 1950s and never thought anything of it, using it to prop open the shed door for the last ten years or so.

"A friend of mine came round recently and got really quite funny about it," said Mrs Johnson, "and it's been on my mind ever since. So I thought I'd better get someone to take a look."

After two visits from police, bomb disposal experts arrived to take away the live munition/doorstop.

The Flying Shed

As gales gusting up to 99mph hit Britain in January 2007 a wooden horse shelter was blown half a mile and ended up in a street in Mossley, Lancashire. Which is better than anything *Brainiac* could manage.

✂ Shed Discovery

A family in Shortlands, near Bromley, found a Romanian man had been living in their garden shed for a month without them realising. Tilly Newman first became suspicious when she saw a figure in the back garden of her home late one night, but assumed that it was their lodger outside.

But the family realised that everything was not as it should be when they woke up the following morning to find a 6" figurine of Jesus placed on the patio.

A few days later while sorting out the garden furniture they found the man camped in the shed. The family believe he had offered the figurine in return for a can of Coca-Cola he had taken.

Ms. Newman told the *Bromley News Shopper* website, "He was drinking a carton of orange juice and then put it in the correct recycling box and it was quite bizarre, almost as if he lived there."

▬▬▬ Shed of Talent

When it was opened in 2007, BBC Scotland's new headquarters was described as appearing on the outside like "a dull and dreary box"… by the BBC website. On the inside it got a bit more interesting with a stepped internal street that rose 95 feet past five floors to the roof area and restaurant.

The £188m building beside the river Clyde in Glasgow has three large studio spaces, with Studio A the largest in Scotland at 8500 square feet.

However the crowning glory is the BBC's acknowledgment that no place really feels like home unless it has a shed. There are also two specially built garden sheds, painted red, and situated on different floors.

"It is a bit of fun and helps to break up the floor space," said Donald Iain Brown, the head of talent. "People can do what they like inside them."

SHED FACT

The Welsh for, "I am going to the shed" is *dwi mynd i'r ysgubor*.

Shed Protection

In 2007 Glasgow police launched a shed protection initiative at Uddingston Flower Festival. Constable Alan Wylie told the *Evening Times*: "The contents of sheds and gardens can amount to a sizeable value and all too often people don't secure those as well as they should." The best crime prevention idea for sheds and gardens won a top prize. Another shed.

 ### Pushing Up The Daisies? No, The Shed

When Aubrey Pilling died just before Christmas in 2008, son Philip decided to save on crematorium fees by burying him underneath a shed in his garden in Bridlington.

One neighbour, who did not wish to be named, told the *Scarborough Evening News*. "It is totally crazy – obviously he's allowed to do it because it's been done, but who would want their dad buried in the garden?"

 ### Blokes 'n' Sheds Fundraiser

Shed crawls are fast becoming a good way to raise money for charity. In 2008 the eighth annual Blokes 'n' Sheds tour in Southland, New Zealand, attracted a strong turnout. The *Southland Times* reported that 160 blokes of all ages took part in the Southland Boys' High School fundraising event, which took them on a mystery tour of five sheds to raise $2000 for the school. Many of the participants had taken part in the previous seven 'bloke' tours.

Organiser Ken Bowie said a lot of the tickets had been bought as Father's Day presents and although "female blokes" were welcome and have come in the past, "none turned up this year".

▬▬— It's Still Standing

The hippy half-brother of Elton John used to live in a shed. Geoff and Reginald (Elton) Dwight are both the sons of former RAF man Stanley Dwight. While Reg went on to become a global superstar, Geoff dropped out of school to become a hippy.

To save money in 1995 he decided to rent out his house and live in a shed in the garden for a year in Hare Krishna simplicity – sleeping on a straw bed and eating vegetables grown by friends. These days he lives in a cottage in Ruthin, Wales, with his partner Karen.

"I've been designing a database capable of holding the whole world's data," he told the *Daily Mail*, "but we were burgled recently, and my laptop and all my work was stolen. So now I'm making *yurts*, which Karen and I turn into amazing fairy spaces at festivals."

With This Ring, I Thee Shed

Beach weddings in the Caribbean have become a lucrative money spinner for tourist resorts from Barbados to Bermuda to the Bahamas, but now another beach resort wants to get a little slice of the action. Bournemouth. Tourism chiefs are hoping that their cream-coloured beach hut may soon be hosting weddings and civil partnerships on Dorset sands.

Head of tourism Mark Smith said, "Bournemouth has always been a very popular resort for weddings and couples have often expressed interest with the hotels for a ceremony on the beach." However, unlike the Caribbean, weddings in England and Wales must take place inside permanent structures, hence the hut. It also takes away the problem of incessant driving rain...

Ice Breaker

Sutton in Surrey is on the flightpath to both Heathrow and Gatwick airports, but when Lloyd Gater heard an ear-splitting crash from his back garden he didn't think it was anything to do with an aircraft. Going out to inspect his back garden, he found his shed smashed, his barbecue flattened and his mower ruined. A block of 'blue ice' the size of a TV set had fallen from a circling plane and deposited itself on Lloyd's outbuilding.

The ice, from an onboard plumbing fault had formed underneath the plane and dropped off as it warmed up on its descent to one of the London airports. Lloyd told *The Sun*, "The crash was enormous, I thought a bomb had gone off."

It's A Cat Jail

A cat which was accidentally locked in a garden shed survived for two months by eating insects and licking condensation off the windows. The black and white cat, known as Emmy, followed its owner into the shed but lingered for too long inside. When he left and locked the door it started a nine-week prison term for the animal – which was given up for dead by its owner. Who then got a very big surprise over two months later…

Shedded Bliss

A vicar is advising couples who get married in his church to buy a shed if they want to remain happily married. The Reverend Jamie Allen of Saint Andrew's at Great Cornard, Suffolk thinks that buying a shed is a serious business and shouldn't be entered into lightly.

"The very act of being in the shed may well be helping men live happily ever after with their wives," he told the *Sunday Mirror*. "The garden shed may give them a safe, private place to unwind and escape the pressure of modern life and marriage."

Signalling a change

SHED FACT

Christopher Parker got fed up with looking at his standard 8 x 6 foot panel shed, so he painted it in the colours of the old Southern Railway, added a few fixtures and fittings and now he has Kenley Signal Box at the bottom of his garden.

SHED FACT

Dave Sandilands runs his licensed tattoo parlour from a shed in his back garden in Girvan, Ayrshire. The service he offers is described as "friendly and private" and the parlour is decked out with all the latest equipment including a hydraulic chair.

A Complicated Plot

A man confessed to the *Guardian* newspaper in 2007 that he'd been living in his allotment shed for ten years. The man – unnamed for NIMBY interventionist purposes – from south-west London needed a garden shed for his allotment and started collecting scrap materials. "Before I knew it, I had built a shed that was bigger than necessary. I was enjoying it more down here than I was in my flat, so I thought, 'Why not give living here a go for a while?'

"It was pretty basic at first – one room with a wood-burning stove. Security wasn't an issue because I had nothing of any value to lose. A lot of the sheds have been broken into, but mine doesn't have a lock, so it never has – it's less tempting.

"That first summer, the council came to see me. I assumed I'd be turfed off, but they didn't seem to give a stuff – they just asked me to lower the roof. From then I started thinking about staying long-term and upgrading. I expanded to two rooms, plastered, painted and added a toilet. There's no electricity and rainwater is collected in a butt, gravity-fed to the sink.

"Because I'm here on my own at night, everything within the gates of the allotments feels like home."

Smallest zoo known to man

SHED FACT

The Zoological Museum, now part of London's Natural History Museum, was begun by Walter Rothschild at the age of seven in a garden shed.

Shed *Lit*

We've had chick lit (literature for chicks), misery lit (literature for people who love to read about other people's misery) and now there is shed lit. Many of our greatest works of fiction have been produced in a shed. George Bernard Shaw, Virginia Woolf, Roald Dahl, Mark Twain, Daphne du Maurier, Philip Pullman and Arthur Miller have all written great works in sheds. Many of the finest novels written in the English language include sheds – Jane Austen included a shed in *Sense and Sensibility*, while Enid Blyton's Secret Seven were always meeting up in the shed…

━━━ The Golden Shed

Author of *Charlie and the Chocolate Factory* and *James and the Giant Peach*, Roald Dahl wrote many of his classic stories in a shed in his garden. He had a battered old wing-backed armchair that he inherited from his mother's house that he would sit in facing the door, along with a board on which he used to write. Dahl would only write in the morning, on yellow legal paper, with a handful of pre-sharpened pencils. His secretary would then type out what he had written by hand and Dahl would edit it later that afternoon.

Describing a typical visit to Dahl's house in the *Guardian* newspaper, long-time collaborator Quentin Blake confessed he was seldom let into Dahl's writing sanctuary. "I didn't go into the shed very often, because the whole point of it as far as Roald was concerned was that it was private. He wrote in the shed as long as I knew him – we worked together for 15 years from 1975 to 1990 and I illustrated a dozen of his books. I would take my drawings down to Gipsy House for him to look at while sitting on the sofa in the dining room."

Dahl also co-wrote the film script for one of the greatest shed movies of all time, *Chitty Chitty Bang Bang*, from an original story by Ian Fleming.

"I turned and retraced my steps to the high, healthy ground; directing them a little aside from my former path, toward a shabby old wooden shed, which stood on the outer skirt of the fir plantation, and which had hitherto been unimportant to share my notice with the wide, wild prospect of the lake. On approaching the shed I found that it had been a boat-house, and that an attempt had apparently been made to convert it afterward into a sort of rude arbor, by placing inside it a fir-wood seat, a few stools and a table."

The Woman in White by Wilkie Collins

Roald Works Ahead

"The table (in the shed) near to his right hand had all kinds of strange memorabilia on it, one of which was a ball of silver paper that he'd collected from bars of chocolate since he was a young man and it had gradually increased in size."

Quentin Blake

Heidegger's Hut

There is a shed connection between Monty Python's Arthur 'Two Sheds' Jackson sketch and their *Bruces' Philosophers Song*. The famous philosophers song – sung in an Australian accent – names the great thinkers of all time including Kant, John Stuart Mill and Wittgenstein (i.e. "Wittgenstein was a beery swine") and tells of the huge quantities of alcohol they liked to consume when they went out philosophising. Hence we get:

> Immanuel Kant was a real pissant
> Who was very rarely stable
> Heidegger, Heidegger was a boozy beggar
> Who could drink you under the table

Martin Heidegger (1889–1976) produced most of his important texts in a mountain hut in the Black Forest, a place he called in straightforward Germanic terms "Die Hutte". From 1922 onwards Heidegger would retreat to his hutte and think deeply about the meaning of life. Martin clearly loved the place, claiming an intellectual and emotional intimacy with the building and its surroundings. Writer Adam Sharr has put together a whole book about Heidegger and his relationship with Die Hutte, which was clearly the inspiration for his key sheddist essay *Building Dwelling Thinking*.

Heidegger was the only philosopher mentioned in the Monty Python song who was still alive at the time, but chose not ta sue. Apart from the fact that the song is not entirely serious, being known as a boozy old sod is a lot better than being a big fan of Hitler from 1933 to 1945.

"By the time I knew Mrs. Ham, her late husband's bank, Cox & Co., had failed and her means were much reduced. Gone was the house on the river at Bourne End and with it the Venetian gondola and gondolier. She had retired to a small Regency house in Totland Bay on the Isle of Wight, where her garden shed, known as 'The Mansion', had been converted into two guest bedrooms. It was dreadfully damp but because it was Mrs. Ham's we loved it."

Wait for Me! by Deborah Mitford, Duchess of Devonshire (and youngest of the six Mitford sisters)

TOP TEN SHED BOOKS

BRIDESHED REVISITED – EVELYN WAUGH

BLEAK OUTHOUSE – CHARLES DICKENS

UNDER THE GREENWOOD TREEHOUSE – THOMAS HARDY

A TALE OF TWO SHEDS JACKSON – CHARLES DICKENS

HOW GREEN WAS MY CHALET – RICHARD LLEWELLYN

WE HAVE TO TALK ABOUT WEATHERING – LIONEL SHRIVER

THE CUT IN THE HUT AND OTHER (POOR WOODWORKING) STORIES – DR. SEUSS

UNCLE TOM'S GARDEN STUDIO – HARRIET BEECHER-STOWE

ROOM AT THE TOP, NEXT TO THE PAINT TINS – JOHN BRAINE

SECRET SHEDS

SECRET SEVEN FIREWORKS
BY ENID BLYTON
"They pulled on coats and tore down the garden to the shed."

WELL DONE, SECRET SEVEN
BY ENID BLYTON
"I got them out of the garden shed, they've been there ages."

SHOCK FOR THE SECRET SEVEN
BY ENID BLYTON
"He tried the handle of the garden shed, but it was locked. He peeped in at the kitchen window."

GO AHEAD SECRET SEVEN
BY ENID BLYTON
"The children began to file in at Peter's gate and make their way down the garden to the shed where the meetings were held."

THE SECRET SEVEN
BY ENID BLYTON
"We could use the old shed at the bottom of the garden for a meeting place, couldn't we."

THREE CHEERS, SECRET SEVEN
BY ENID BLYTON
"Jack went to his garden shed to see if there was a ladder there."

GOOD OLD SECRET SEVEN
BY ENID BLYTON
"They meet in the old shed at the bottom of the garden and you can't get in if you don't know the password! They've even made badges."

SECRET SEVEN ON THE TRAIL
BY ENID BLYTON
"By five o'clock every single member of the Secret Seven was in the shed in Peter's garden."

LOOK OUT SECRET SEVEN
BY ENID BLYTON
"They ran down the garden to the meeting shed."

✂ To The Outhouse...

Virginia Woolf typified every writer that ever sought refuge in a shed to practice their art. The celebrated author of *Mrs Dalloway* (1925), *To the Lighthouse* (1927) and *Orlando* (1928), wrote in *A Room of One's Own* (1929), "A woman must have money and a room of her own if she is to write fiction."

Virginia's was a converted toolshed in the garden of her home at Rodmel in Sussex, placed in a vantage point that looked out across the South Downs and the Ouse Valley.

At first she would write there only in summer and was only forced inside by the chill of autumn; though she would sometimes persist until it was too cold to hold a pen. In 1924 she got an oil heater and was able to extend the time spent in a shed of her own.

Woolf referred to her place of work as the "Writing Lodge" and in 1934 it was moved away from its original position to a spot at the far end of the garden, under a chestnut tree and closer to the neighbouring churchyard wall. Parts of all her major novels were written in the building that is today preserved by the National Trust, along with her desk, diaries and the lamp that she used to write by in the winter months.

It was here that she wrote her final words one spring morning in 1941, a suicide letter addressed to her husband Leonard, before loading her overcoat pockets with stones and walking into the river Ouse.

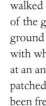

"When he heard the gate bang, he turned round and walked down the path towards a shed at the bottom of the garden. In front of the shed a small square of ground had been covered with pebbles and bordered with white-washed bricks, set into the soil side by side, at an angle. The roof and sides of the shed had been patched neatly with lengths of tarpaulin. The door had been freshly painted, and a square had been sawn out the top half and barred vertically with clean laths. On a shelf behind the bars stood a kestrel hawk."

A Kestrel For A Knave by Barry Hines

"She had been heard to say that at least there was one of 'em at Cold Comfort as knew her own mind, even if she 'ad seen something nasty in the woodshed when she was two. Flora had no idea what this last sentence could possibly mean. Possibly it was a local idiom for going cuckoo."

Cold Comfort Farm by Stella Gibbons

83

When Dr. Cowan paid £5 for a garage set on the cliff near his Laugharne Boat House, in a beautiful spot overlooking the Taf estuary, he had no idea that it would eventually become the workplace of the country's finest poet and a place of pilgrimage.

Dylan's "Wordsplashed Hut"

Dylan Thomas's writing shed started out in life as a garage for Dr. Cowan's Wolseley. Dr. Cowan owned the Boat House at Laugharne in the 1920s, but it was not until 1948 that Thomas's great friend Margaret Taylor – wife of historian A.J.P. Taylor – found the house looking out onto a tidal estuary and bought it for him. Writing to thank her Thomas declared, "All I write in this water and tree room on the cliff, every word will be a thanks to you." Caitlin and Dylan Thomas moved into the property in May 1949. The room was already fitted out with an anthracite-fuelled stove, two tables and a bookcase. Thomas called it his "wordsplashed hut" and he had magazine and newspaper cuttings pinned to the walls. It was here that he wrote one of his famous poems, "Do not go gentle into that good night", written for a father dying of cancer.

His writing routine was unlike most writers in that he pottered his way through a morning before walking into town and drinking at the Brown's Hotel to catch up with town gossip. Then he would return to his "study, atelier, or bard's bothy" looking out on the Taf estuary and write from two till seven. Caitlin Thomas recalled "at the end of an intensive five hour stretch, prompt as clockwork, Dylan would come out very pleased with himself saying he had done a good day's work, and present me proudly with one or two, or three perhaps, fiercely belaboured lines".

"For where the old thick laurels grow, along the thin red wall, you find the tool and potting sheds, which are the heart of all."

Rudyard Kipling

"She saw a secret little clearing, and a secret little hut made of rustic poles. And she had never been here before! She realised it was the quiet place where the growing pheasants were reared; the keeper in his shirt-sleeves was kneeling, hammering."

Lady Chatterley's Lover by D.H. Lawrence

"From this same spot your power was spread
Here stood the first rude wooden shed
Here first a ditch was cut on shore
Where now they ply the splashing oar."

Faust by Johann Wolfgang von Goethe

"The hut was quite cozy, panelled with unvarnished deal, having a little rustic table and stool beside his chair, and a carpenter's bench, then a big box, tools, new boards, nails; and many things hung from pegs: axe, hatchet, traps, things in sacks, his coat. It had no window, the light came in through the open door. It was a jumble, but also it was a sort of little sanctuary."

Lady Chatterley's Lover by D.H. Lawrence

GBS and The Revolver

Playwright George Bernard Shaw's retreat to his writing shed was as much about getting away from the world as finding somewhere to write. He had bought a rectory in the Hertfordshire village of Ayot St. Lawrence at the age of 50, in 1906, (he lived till 1950) and eventually took over his wife Charlotte's summer house to write in. Apart from giving him the isolation he yearned for, it allowed the servants to say with all honesty that, "Mr. Shaw is out" when visitors called. He once complained that he couldn't stick his head out of the window of the house without being photographed.

Shaw's tiny shed was unlike any other writer's retreat in that it revolved. In winter it could be turned to follow the sun during the day, giving the maximum amount of light and warmth, and in summer, away from the sun to give him cool and shade.

Although it was very much his writing hut, it was built in the 1920s long after his acclaimed works such as *Pygmalion* (1912) and *Man and Superman* (1902) had been published. Shaw hated the cold and an electric cable was run out to the writing hut to run an electric fire and also a telephone cable with a buzzer to tell him when lunch was ready. Though he often ignored it.

After his death in 1950 the house was gifted to the National Trust. His beloved writing hut was renovated by the University of Hertfordshire who got it revolving again.

Nancy Astor once banged on the door of Shaw's shed, saying: "Come out of there, you old fool. You've written enough nonsense in your life!"

"'He intends to send his groom into Somersetshire immediately for it,' she added, 'and when it arrives, we will ride every day. You shall share its use with me. Imagine to yourself, my dear Elinor, the delight of a gallop on some of these downs.'

Most unwilling was she to awaken from such a dream of felicity, to comprehend all the unhappy truths which attended the affair, and for some time she refused to submit to them. As to an additional servant, the expense would be a trifle; mama, she was sure, would never object to it; and any horse would do for him; he might always get one at the Park; as to a stable, the merest shed would be sufficient."

Sense and Sensibility by Jane Austen

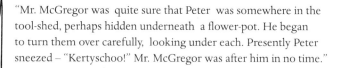

"Mr. McGregor was quite sure that Peter was somewhere in the tool-shed, perhaps hidden underneath a flower-pot. He began to turn them over carefully, looking under each. Presently Peter sneezed – "Kertyschoo!" Mr. McGregor was after him in no time."

The Tale of Peter Rabbit by Beatrix Potter

His Roofing Materials

Author of *Northern Lights*, *The Subtle Knife* and *The Amber Spyglass* Philip Pullman was well known for writing in a shed. Interviewed in 1998 he described his writing ritual in the shed.

"It's quite comfortable in there, but because of my superstition about not tidying it during the course of a book, it's now an abominable tip. I write by hand, using a ballpoint pen on narrow lined A4 paper (with two holes, not four). I sit at a table covered with an old kilim rug, on a vastly expensive Danish orthopaedic chair, which has made a lot of difference to my back. The table is raised on wooden blocks so it's a bit higher than normal.

However, interviewed by *The Economist* magazine in 2007 Pullman revealed that having finished *His Dark Materials* trilogy and having won countless awards he was no longer writing in the garden.

"I used to work in a shed in my garden. But it got too crowded with books and manuscripts and all kinds of bits and pieces, and I got fed up with being down at the end of the garden, especially on rainy days; and then we moved house anyway, and I had to decide whether to take the shed with us or leave it there. In the end I gave it to a friend, the illustrator Ted Dewan – on condition that when he's finished with it, he'll give it to another writer. He's replaced the windows and some of the roof, and I like the idea that it'll get passed on to lots of other writers and illustrators, and each of them will replace this bit or that bit until there isn't an atom of the original shed left."

SHED FACT

Daphne du Maurier wrote *My Cousin Rachel* in a shed in Cornwall in the winter of 1949. It was in the garden of a large country house called Menabilly which she rented from 1943 till 1967.

Mark Twain's Pilot House

Mark Twain produced many of his greatest works in a small octagonal wooden hut 12 feet across (pictured below). It was perched high on a hill in Elmira, New York state and said to resemble the pilot house of a Mississippi riverboat. Twain lived his early life as Samuel Clemens in Hannibal, Missouri, on the banks of the Mississippi river and trained as a riverboat pilot on the 1000 miles of river between St Louis and New Orleans. His pen name was the sounding depth for six feet; "Mark Twain!" After studying the shoals and shifting islands of America's great river for three years as a young man, the Civil War brought trade on the Mississippi to a standstill and Clemens headed west, eventually falling into his first writing job on the *San Francisco Chronicle*.

"It is the loveliest study you ever saw…octagonal with a peaked roof, each face filled with a spacious window… perched in complete isolation on the top of an elevation that commands leagues of valley and city and retreating ranges of distant blue hills. It is a cozy nest and just room in it for a sofa, table, and three or four chairs, and when the storms sweep down the remote valley and the lightning flashes behind the hills beyond and the rain beats upon the roof over my head – imagine the luxury of it."

Mark Twain

The Frog Cabin

Mark Twain's 'pilot house' wasn't the first shed he wrote in. The novelist and travel writer was propelled to national attention by his short story *The Celebrated Jumping Frog of Calaveras County*, which was first published in *The Saturday Press* and *The Californian* in 1865. Encouraged by its reception he wrote a collection of 27 short stories which appeared under that name in 1867.

After turning his back on riverboat piloting, Twain had taken up as a miner in Nevada. He first heard the frog tale while staying at the log cabin of the Gillis brothers at the top of Jackass Hill at Angel's Camp in California. He spent three months there at the end of the Civil War, mining, visiting neighbouring towns and sitting round the old smoke stack swapping tales. He then wrote up the short story in the cabin and its publication changed his life.

Original 1956 caption: "World-famous playwright Arthur Miller, author of *Death of a Salesman* and other hits, is shown in a reflective mood as he sits in the workshop he built himself on the grounds of his Connecticut home. Miller, a very handy guy with tools, does most of his writing in this small building."

Arthur 'One Shed' Miller

Playwright Arthur Miller built a shed in which to write one of his greatest ever plays, *Death of a Salesman*. He had just had the first flush of success with *All My Sons* on Broadway in 1947 and bought a house near Roxbury, Connecticut. He had an idea to write a play about a salesman but needed an undisturbed space to do it in. In the woods, at some distance from the house, he built the clapboard cabin. "It was a purely instinctive act," he told author and *New Yorker* columnist John Lahr, "I had never built a building in my life." As Miller constructed the shed he turned over the material for the play in his mind. So much was ready to flood out that when he finally got his desk placed in the shed (made from an old door) he wrote the first act in a day. *Death of a Salesman* (1949) won a Tony, a New York Drama Critics Award and a Pulitzer Prize, the first play to win all three.

The shed is still standing today, little changed from when Miller knocked it together.

"'No... no!' screamed Aunt Ada Doom, on a high note that always cracked with her agony. 'I cannot bear it. There have always been Starkadders at Cold Comfort. You mustn't go... none of you must go... I shall go mad. I saw something nasty in the woodshed... Ah... ah... ah...'"

Cold Comfort Farm by Stella Gibbons

"'And here's Major Benjy,' said Miss Mapp, who had made her slip about his Christian name yesterday, and had been duly entreated to continue slipping. 'And Captain Puffin. Well, that is nice! Shall we go into my little garden shed, dear Mrs Poppit, and have our Tea?'"

Lucia Rising by E.F. Benson

Henry David Thoreau was one of the earliest shed writers, but he decided to spend two years in a hut near Walden Pond in Concord, Massachusetts not because of interruptions, but because he wanted to see what it would be like to live the simple life, close to nature.

"I went to the woods because I wished to live deliberately, to front only the essential facts of life, and see if I could not learn what it had to teach, and not, when I came to die, discover that I had not lived."

He built his 10 x 15 foot hut himself on land owned by the writer Ralf Waldo Emerson and retreated there for two years, making notes in his journal, greeting the occasional woodcutter or itinerant labourer passing through. Including the costs of construction of his home and the food for his first year, his household expenditure for 1845 was $28.12.

In that time he came up with what could be the creed for shed owners everywhere:

"I never found the companion that was so companionable as solitude."

Walden, or *Life in the Woods* was published in 1854 and has, over successive generations, been elevated to the level of American classic. The book which features Thoreau's two years compressed into four seasons, is part social experiment, part voyage of spiritual discovery, and also a manual for self reliance.

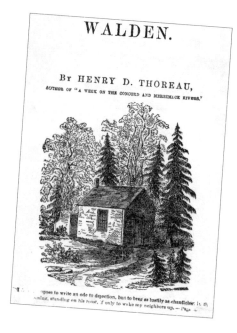

The spirit of Thoreau lives on. Tumbleweed, a company in America, has taken the concept of Thoreau's hut and designed a series of tiny wooden houses, with a bunk up above and living quarters below. They have hoisted this onto a trailer, so you can take your tiny house wherever you wish – maybe into the woods like Thoreau. Pictured above is a recreation of Thoreau's hut close to where it originally stood in Massachusetts.

The Van Helsing Of Sheds

Best-selling author Robert Harris: "I am anti-sheddist. I couldn't work anywhere cold and nasty. I like the background noise of life going on."

> "'I saw something nasty in the woodshed!' screamed Aunt Ada Doom, flapping about her with something which Flora recognised as all that was left of the *Cowkeepers' Weekly Bulletin and Milk Producer's Guide.*"
>
> *Cold Comfort Farm* by Stella Gibbons

One in a tower

SHED FACT

Author and conservationist Laurens van der Post, when living at Aldeburgh, Suffolk, in the 1980s, would walk five minutes from his house to write in a disused coastguards' tower.

Pheasant Watching With Louis de Bernieres

Author of *Captain Corelli's Mandolin*, Louis de Bernieres, is an advocate of working from a shed. At his home on the Suffolk/Norfolk border he has a summerhouse with all the home comforts. Solar panels supply power for his lights, laptop and music system, while he is heated in spring, autumn and winter by calor gas.

"Anyone who works at home needs a refuge from the rest of the household, as far from the house as possible, and definitely without a phone." He told the *Guardian* in their long-running Writers' Rooms series. "It is nice to look up and see the pheasants strutting about outside, but the best thing about the shed is its absolutely quintessential smell of sheds."

The downside of working in the garden was that his laptop got stolen from his shed. He thought he had lost the first 50 pages of *A Partisan's Daughter* when his shed was broken into.

"Eventually, the laptop turned up in a ditch near Bungay, but I didn't get it back for four months. I had contacted Norfolk police and it had been handed in to Suffolk police. It was only returned because someone had the bright idea of turning it on and found the opening chapters."

> "I love Edinburgh. It has one of the best tool shops in the country, Murray's. I asked that man to adopt me, because I like his tools. If you lead a fairly intellectual sitting-on-your-bum kind of life you need to have lots of concrete experiences as well, so I do carpentry and joinery. I'm building a lean-to on the back of my shed; I like repairing broken things, it just keeps me relatively normal, I think."
>
> Louis de Bernieres in *The Scotsman*

Shed *Facts*

There are many astonishing shed facts that astound and delight in equal measure. They include the things that women prefer to call a shed, but avoiding the word 'shed', the percentage of serious injuries that occur in a shed, the rich variety of wildlife that will try to make a home in your shed, the Australian state with the most valuable sheds and the English county that has the biggest sheds. Given that 52% of the population own a shed it's no surprise that many celebrities have got one, but we name the celebs who are proud to consider themselves Sheddies, including Hollywood's finest character actor.

Shed Fact: Built By Amish

Lancaster County Barns have a unique selling point when it comes to their range of quality storage sheds and equine outbuildings. They are all built by Amish craftsmen. "The reputation of the Amish for quality workmanship is based on reality, not myth. Aspects of Amish culture—a strong work ethic, values rooted in integrity rather than show, a tradition of expertise in woodwork and craftsmanship—all contribute to the consistently high quality of Amish-made products."

And they do sell to the English.

Shed Fact: Covered Bridges

Covered bridges look like drive-through sheds. The Roseman covered bridge, in rural Iowa, dates to 1883 and was the star of *The Bridges of Madison County*. Americans built sheds over their bridges to preserve the wooden trusses and spars underneath – a covered bridge could last 80 years longer than an uncovered one. And in a country that had a lot of trees it didn't take much to knock up a nice little shed on top of the bridge.

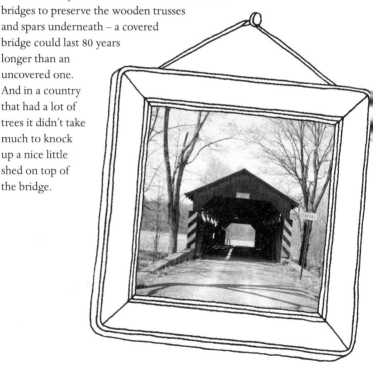

GIVE A SHED A BAD NAME

THE THINGS PEOPLE CALL THEIR SHED HIDEAWAYS

Keel Hall

The Hobbit Hole

The Duck and Dumper

The Silver Spur Saloon

Lockett Inn

Eric the Dancing Shed

Cherise's Marmalade Cottage

Two Sheds From Heaven

Blenheim

The Shed-We-Like

Frankenshed

The Ruminator

House of Fallen Timbers

Jabba The Hut

✂ Shed Fact: Much Older Than Wednesday

Sheffield F.C. is officially recognised by FIFA as the oldest football club in the world. The club started up on 24th October, 1857, and based itself in a potting shed for the first few years of its existence. Despite its head start in the game it failed to keep pace with rivals Sheffield United and the team that played on Wednesdays.

✂ Shed Fact: Britain's Oldest Beach Hut

Bournemouth Council are proud possessors of Britain's oldest beach hut. Hut No. 2359 has been given its own blue plaque to commemorate a century in existence. It was constructed in 1909 and still has its original structural foundations, with what the Bournemouth Beach Office describe as "just a few maintenance updates". So, this plucky beach hut has seen out World War I, resisted the Luftwaffe and survived the package holiday boom of the 1970s. The plaque was unveiled by a hut tenant of 20 years, Mrs. Jean Smith, who the *Bournemouth Echo* described as a "seaside enthusiast".

The Shed At Night

"My grandparents lived in Selsey so I spent a lot of time there as a kid. I remember seeing Patrick Moore driving around the village in a beaten up old Triumph 2000 and hearing him coming from miles away on his squeaky old pushbike.

"There was a guy living opposite who owned a really big telescope, at least it seemed big when I was knee high to a grasshopper. Patrick used to visit him. It was in a bright green shed in the garden that swivelled on a track. My dad thought he was going mad the first few times we went to see my grandparents and the shed door was in a different position each time!"

'CureforSanity', *Sky at Night* magazine

Shed Fact: Calendar Sheds

The amazingly successful, alternative W.I. calendar from the Yorkshire W.I., which has raised close on £2 million for Leukaemia Research, ventured into the potting shed for their 2010 reprise. The now-famous calendar girls chose 12 new scenarios for their ten-year anniversary, and a shed was a winning choice. Here, the potting shed appears as Miss April, along with Lynda Logan.

SHED FACT

If it were large enough, 6% of people would contemplate transforming their shed into a bar or club.

THE TOP 20 THINGS FOUND IN A SHED

1. Spade, forks and other garden tools
2. Garden chairs
3. Bicycles and bicycle equipment
4. Lawn mower
5. Herbicides, pesticides, insecticides, slug pellets
6. Sundry garden appliances, hoses
7. Barbecue
8. Foldable table
9. Parasol
10. Paintbrushes
11. Paint
12. Power tools
13. Sports equipment
14. Spare DIY tools
15. Children's toys
16. Wood offcuts
17. Pet paraphernalia
18. An inherited object that can't be thrown away
19. Tubers, corms or bulbs that have to overwinter there
20. Smelly pet food

TOP TEN WILDLIFE FOUND IN SHEDS

1. Spiders
2. Mice
3. Rats
4. Cats
5. Wasps
6. Hedgehogs
7. Birds
8. Bats
9. Dogs
10. Snakes

SHED FACT

In Ukrainian folklore 'The Raspberry Hut' tells of a giant raspberry which, when cut in half, opens to reveal a bright room inside. The giant raspberry is in fact a hut, or shed.

Shed Fact: Lock The Door And The Roof

Jack Sutcliffe from retailer TigerSheds.com has revealed that many of the shed owners he deals with, who have had a shed broken into, are surprised at the thieves' approach. "We often get orders from customers who have had a previous shed vandalised or broken into. The feedback we have received is that most acts of theft come from taking the roof of the shed off, rather than entering through a door or window."

 ### Shed Fact: ...And All That Jazz

In jazz parlance 'to woodshed' or 'shed' is understood as 'shutting oneself away from the rest of the world to practice' as in 'going to the woodshed'.

 ### Shed Fact: They're Just Like Us

While your Russian oligarchs like to decamp to Monaco and the South of France aboard their £10 million yachts, the Queen and Prince Philip have spent summers enjoying their Norfolk beach hut. The hut, in woodland near Sandringham, overlooking a stretch of Norfolk coastline had been used by the royal family for 70 years. Prince Philip had been known to cook barbecues on the small verandah. Sadly, it was burnt down by vandals in 2003.

Shed Values: Wales On Top

Almost 40% of people consider a shed to be an important factor when buying a house. The average UK value for a shed comes in at £508 with over 17% of shed owners having sheds valued in excess of £1000. Welsh shed owners are believed to invest the most in their outbuildings with 36% of owners valuing their sheds at over £1000.

10 CELEBRITY SHEDDIES

1. Heston Blumenthal

2. Sarah Beeney (Star judge of the Cuprinol/Shedblog Shed of the Year competition)

3. Jamie Oliver

4. Vic Reeves

5. Chris Evans

6. Morgan Freeman

7. Trinny and Susannah

8. Terry Jones (Arthur 'Two Sheds' Jackson)

9. James May

10. Patrick Moore

David Gilmour of Pink Floyd couldn't be included because his shed had to be removed. This is the offending item. Talk about rock star excess...

SHED SALES: THE INSIDE STORY

Top UK shed retailer Tiger Sheds answered some pretty ferocious questioning (think Jeremy Paxman/John Humphrys) about their shed retail business. The results of this relentless probing give an insight into what kind of sheds are springing up all over Britain and the bungling that goes on when putting them together.

WHAT IS THE SMALLEST SHED YOU SELL?

Our cheapest is one of our smallest sheds – The Tiger Overlap Toolroom (3 x 3 foot) This is currently £139.99 which includes VAT and delivery.

MOST EXPENSIVE SHED?

Our most expensive (and largest) shed would be one of our log cabins. The (30 x 18 foot) Omega Log Cabin is £6049.99.

YOUR TOP-FIVE BEST-SELLING GARDEN SHEDS/POTTING SHEDS/WOODEN WORKSHOP SHEDS?

1. Shiplap Apex (four window panels and a three-hinge door)
2. Shiplap Pent (classic pent-style shed with quality tongue and groove shiplap cladding)
3. Overlap Apex – (featuring 9mm overlap cladding)
4. Pent Bike Store – (extra large double doors for easy bike access)
5. Apex Bike Shed (superior grade 12mm shiplap cladding)

8 x 6 foot is by far the most popular size shed followed by the 7 x 5 foot and then the 6 x 4 foot.

WHAT PROPORTION OF SHEDS DO YOU ERECT FOR THE CUSTOMER?

Approximately 10% of our customers pay for our installation service. All of our panels are pre-assembled and the door is pre-hung which does make installation, for those who are up for it, fairly easy. Plus there are plenty of videos on the website to assist.

MOST EXPENSIVE SHED ACCESSORY?

This would probably be our solar light at £49.99. Our log cabins come with many expensive extras such as deck additions, roof shingles, guttering etc.

HOW MANY DIFFERENT SHEDS DO YOU SUPPLY?

We have a range of approximately 60 different styles of sheds. However, because each shed comes in various sizes, we actually offer over 300 buildings. And that's not to mention our bespoke offerings.

ARE PEOPLE ORDERING BIGGER AND GRANDER SHEDS AS THE YEARS GO BY?

We find as the years go by that people go more for log cabins rather than large garden sheds. I think this trend will continue to grow as more and more people become aware of the interlocking log cabin. With the internet and all the choice available we find that the demand for an exact size is increasing where people want a shed that fits perfectly in a specific place in their garden. I think more and more people are now looking for specific sizes and not simply the standard 8 x 6 foot shed, rather than simply going for bigger and grander sheds.

WHAT'S THE AVERAGE LENGTH OF A SHED'S LIFE?

Providing the customer looks after their shed – seals in the windows, re-treats the shed every year, stops anything from becoming in contact with the shed (e.g. overhanging branches), checks and replaces felt, lubricates the hinges etc, then a shed can last 25–30 years.

WHAT PROPORTION OF SHEDS HAVE THE TRADITIONAL FELT ROOF?

All of our sheds would come with traditional felt as standard. We do offer the customer the chance to upgrade to premium roof shingles if they wish. Not many people do unless it is a log cabin.

WHAT'S THE MOST-REPORTED PROBLEM WITH A NEW SHED? (I.E. LEAKY ROOF, WINDOW DOESN'T FIT, DOOR DOESN'T CLOSE ETC)

Surprisingly one of the most common problems that people complain about is that a shed looks twisted or out of position, and the door doesn't close properly. However, it is generally the case that this stems from an uneven base. We often find that the customer never believes us when we tell them they have an uneven base and they are adamant that the shed is wrong. We advise them to put small packing blocks under opposite corners of the building and it generally seems to do the trick.

ARE THERE ANY TRENDS IN SHED SALES?

Yes, apart from the obvious trend that it is busy in the summer and quiet in the winter, there are two real peaks in shed sales. One is when it starts to get warm (near Easter, coinciding with the bank holidays in April/May) which we find is very busy for shed sales. There is then a second peak towards the end of the summer as people see it as the last chance to get a shed up before the weather gets bad again.

HOW OLD ARE SHED DESIGNS?

Despite very minor changes over the years (which come from making manufacturing easier rather than improving the design/aesthetics) the general designs of most of our buildings have been around for approximately 25 years, since our manufacturing unit began.

WHAT PROPORTION OF WOMEN BUY SHEDS?

Many of our customers are female, probably 30–40% of our customers.

ARE THERE ANY REGIONAL TRENDS OR ODDITIES IN SHED SALES?

Far more sheds are sold in Cornwall than Devon. People in Yorkshire buy bigger sheds than any other county in the UK.

HAVE YOU HAD ANY SHED ERECTION DISASTER STORIES YOU
KNOW OF – FOR EXAMPLE, PEOPLE WHO HAVE PUT THE ROOF
ON UPSIDE DOWN?

We sometimes find customers who complain their side
walls are a few inches too short on each side, only to discover
they have put their roof on the floor. We tend to never hear
from these people again after they realise their mistake!
I would say the worst (or at least most annoying 'disaster')
is when the shed is delivered to a customer's house, for the
customer to find the panels won't fit through their house
into the back garden. And they believe this is our fault!

DO YOU HAVE A TOP SHED ERECTION TIP?

Without a doubt, a firm and level base is the key to the
longevity of a shed.

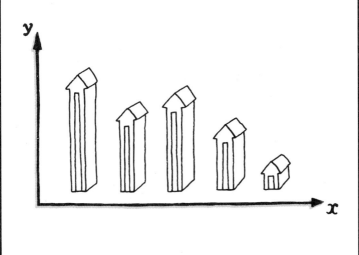

The £250,000 Shed

In June 2011 estate agents started marketing
Britain's most expensive small building. The
beach hut pictured below is in the picturesque
Devon fishing village of Shaldon with views out
to sea and across the River Teign. For your quarter
of a million quid you get a property measuring
just 23 x 6 feet, fitted with an expensive solid
oak door, top of the range kitchen units and
appliances. Then there are add-on wall cabinets
with discreet lighting, under-floor heating, a
staircase to a sleeping area, a marble tiled wet
room, sun terrace and steps down to the beach.

AUSSIE SHEDS: THE FACTS

In 2009 Bankwest conducted a nationwide survey of Aussie sheds: who used them, what was kept in them and what was their proudest achievement in them. Unlike the Brits, Aussie males like to get out there and make stuff in their sheds. But 10% of households said that the primary user was actually female.

* ★ 12% encouraged their partner to go off to the shed
* ★ 2% resented them going off to the shed
* ★ 76% didn't mind
* ★ 8% didn't know what their partner's opinion was about them going off to the shed

 Western Australian Women Are The Most Understanding

When it came to female partners understanding the need for men to have a shed of their own, 50% of women from Western Australia understood the place it had in their man's life. Whereas women in New South Wales were least understanding at 34%.

SHED FACT

* 16% of Aussie shed users have had a serious accident in their shed. This is very similar to British shed users, where 20% of shed users have had an accident in theirs.
* 2% of Aussie shed accidents resulted in long-term damage to the shed owner.

✂ The Joy of Sheds?

Aussies, when they're in the shed, don't necessarily enjoy themselves. When asked if they enjoyed the time spent in their shed 19% said they always enjoyed it, 46% usually enjoyed it, 26% sometimes enjoyed it and 9% got no enjoyment from it at all.

Looking back at the question it was indeed about the joy of sheds and not the joy of sex.

▬◄ Proudest Achievement In A Shed

A whopping 63% of Australians have made something in their shed, with the most likely object being an item of furniture at 20%. When asked if anyone had ever made jewellery in the shed the answer came back – 0%.

◄ Shed Values

The most valuable Aussie sheds (and their contents) are in Queensland where owners value their sheds at an average of A$10,586; New South Wales is next at A$9,398; while in Western Australia sheds are valued on average at A$4,166.

NASTY SPIDERS FOUND IN AUSTRALIAN SHEDS

* Red-back spider – highly venomous / can be deadly – prefers dry habitats; is often found in outhouses.

* White-tail spider – venomous and highly dangerous – prefers cool moist locations and is commonly found in garden mulch areas, but will wander into buildings in the summer to escape the heat.

* Black-house spider – venomous, causes nausea – prefers dry habitat areas and secluded locations, commonly found in sheds.

* Huntsman spider – low risk and non-aggressive – often found indoors, prefers the roof spaces of buildings.

World, you can go to blazes

SHED FACT

28% of Australian shed-owners consider their shed a refuge from the world.

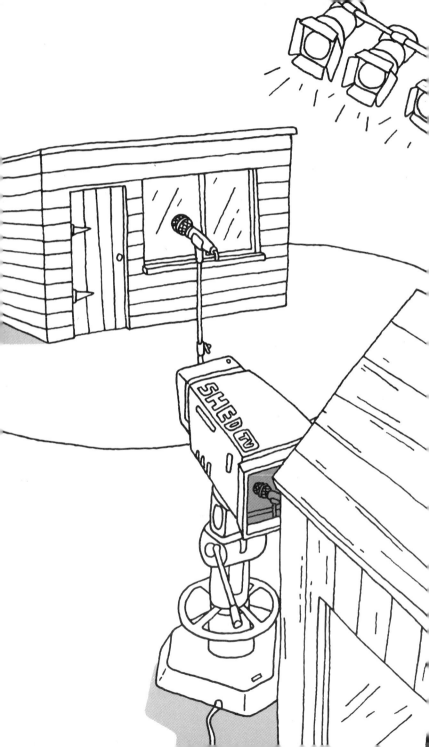

Shed *TV*

Like any small space portrayed on television, sheds suffer from the fact that they're too small to be filmed in. So while barns and stables can play major roles as TV locations, the shed or the cabin of a motorboat, is rarely more than a bitpart player. When they do appear on the box they are ludicrously large in scale, if filmed on the inside, or confined to an exterior shot with characters emerging or disappearing into the shed. *The Fast Show* was notable for having three separate shed strands, while *Top Gear's* Richard Hammond seems hell-bent on destroying as many sheds as he can for comedy value – whichever programme he's working on.

Arthur's 'Uncle Ned'

Sheds, being part of the national fabric, turn up on our best-loved soaps. By their very nature they are buildings where solitary activity takes place – plus they're so nadgy to film in – so they don't appear as often as they deserve. However the exception was the shed of *EastEnders'* Arthur Fowler.

Loving husband of Pauline, father of Tucker from *Grange Hill*, Arthur would use his allotment shed as a refuge. After a bit of Christmas Club embezzling or an argument with Pauline he would disappear down his "Uncle Ned" to brew some tea and contemplate where it all went wrong. The *EastEnders* scriptwriters did everything they could to 'sex up' Arthur's shed – there were storylines about growing cannabis, clandestine sex and *Blue Peter* garden-style mindless vandalism. They didn't manage to bury someone beneath it – but surely the Mitchell brothers would have got round to that sooner or later, had not Arthur died from injuries he sustained in a prison riot. The much-loved character slipped away peacefully in his much-loved shed.

Last Of The Summer Wine

If ever there was a television programme that could be counted on to have its fair share of sheds in, then that would be *Last of the Summer Wine*. The programme ran for 31 series between 1973 and 2010 featuring Compo, Clegg and Foggy and an untold number of bicycles. In Series 17, which went out on the BBC in autumn 1995, there was an episode titled 'The Thing in Wesley's Shed'. Wesley Pegden (actor Gordon Wharmby) is busy creating a secret invention in his shed and the trio set out to discover what it is. They have a fair idea it's a machine of some ilk after they help carry some motor parts back to the shed, but he won't let them inside. When it's time for Wesley to test his contraption, the men persuade Eli to give them a lift in his car so they can follow Wesley. But Eli's driving is atrocious and they end up in a haystack. As ever. It turns out that in a bid to impress Nora Batty, Wesley has invented what he thinks is an amphibious car. But it sinks. Who could have seen that one coming?

Crossroads Shed Action

It's not exactly Corrie's tram crash and explosion, or the Dales' plane falling out of the sky and devastating a village, but in a 2001 episode of *Crossroads* Phil (actor Neil Granger) risked his life in a desperate bid to rescue Scott from Bradley's shed when it went up in flames.

Frank Sidebottom's Fantastic Shed Show

Wacky Frank Sidebottom – the bloke with the *papier mache* head and the grating, nasal Mancunian accent – invited guests into his shed for a programme that redefined the phrase 'shoestring budget'. Only six programmes were ever made of *Frank Sidebottom's Fantastic Shed Show*, with Caroline Aherne playing Mrs Merton and Radio 2's Mark Radcliffe (right) appearing as Emmerson 'Emmo' Lake.

Like taking a holiday...

SHED FACT

In their survey of sheds and shed habits, Cuprinol found that 77% of men have access to a shed and a man spends almost seven days in his shed over the course of the year – presumably justifying all that expenditure on timber preservation applications.

And So Their Work Was Done

Some of Britain's most cherished children's television characters came to life in a shed. The animators Oliver Postgate and Peter Firmin created *Noggin the Nog*, *Pogles Wood*, *Ivor the Engine*, *Clangers* and *Bagpuss*. And all from a shed owned by Peter Firmin.

Channel 4 ran a documentary on the partners in 1997. It turns out that the *Clangers* were only coloured pink because that was the colour of wool that Joan Firmin had handy. *Bagpuss* was supposed to be a marmalade cat, but while he was being made the colour ran and he became pink as well.

After Oliver Postgate's death in 2008, Peter Firmin found almost 40 rusty reels of videotape buried deep in one of Postgate's own sheds. They contained a priceless collection of *Ivor the Engine* episodes shot in black and white in the 1960s. The collection is being digitised and re-released.

Pictured above is the original 'Bagpuss, dear Bagpuss, Old fat furry catpuss' with Emily Firmin in 1974. Only 13 episodes of the show were ever made.

A Shed For Sport Relief

The *Top Gear* team of Jeremy Clarkson, James May and Richard Hammond evoked memories of the golden age of silent comedy when they attempted a *Ground Force* transformation of Sir Steve Redgrave's garden in 2008. In the original *Ground Force* programme, Allan Titchmarsh, Charlie Dimmock and Tommy Walsh would arrive and transform some lucky punter's garden from a herbaceous wasteland to a horticultural oasis. For Sport Relief, the *Top Gear* team turned up and turned the former Olympic rower's garden from a pleasant open space into a wasteland.

True to his love of sheds, James May, complete with a Polish workforce, managed to erect a shed for Sir Steve only to see it demolished in a series of set-piece comedy moments not out of place in *Last of the Summer Wine*.

May's shed was first destroyed by Richard Hammond's digger, rebuilt and blown over by an explosive blast from Jeremy Clarkson trying to destroy the original rockery. The shed was rebuilt and then flattened by some rugby posts falling on it and finally set on fire by Richard Hammond's innovative jet engine barbecue.

The only element of the garden that Sir Steve was pleased with – the greenhouse – was destroyed when Clarkson switched on his over-engineered water feature, which blew the top off itself and crashed through the glass. All they needed was Nora Batty.

The Saturn V Shed

Like caravans, pianos and Morris Marinas, sheds suffer the indignity of being a cheap and easy object of comedy destruction. Richard Hammond's *Brainiac* programme is fond of disposing of them and in one series of the science experimentation show decided to send one 'into space'.

Rocket-FX.com were commissioned by the programme makers to take one small step for mankind by sending an outbuilding into orbit. They took a standard 6 x 4 foot apex shed, purchased from a popular DIY chain, and internally reinforced it with wooden spars. A wood and fibreglass structure was built into the roof to hold six large solid fuel rocket engines. A plywood skirt was added around the outer edge of the shed to make it aerodynamically stable.

Vic Reeves, himself a shed writer, had the honour of pushing the GO button for the maiden voyage of 'Space Shed 2000 XL'. Under 400kg of thrust she flew to an astonishing altitude before turning over, and crashing back down onto the runway. Space was not quite achieved, but witnesses believe she got to 250 feet.

Corrie's Shed Action

It was typical of *Coronation Street*'s writers that they should spurn the sex/crime intrigue of Arthur Fowler's shed and go for the comedy angle of Jack Duckworth. After turning up at the Duckworth's, son Terry is not pleased that Jack and Vera have decided he can live in their shed. That is, until he sees how comfortable Jack has made it...

Adam Buxton – Alone In The Shed

Comedian Adam Buxton (of Adam and Joe fame) was much taken with the 2009 Channel 4 documentary *Alone in the Wild*. "Ed Wardle set off to the Canadian Yukon to see how long he could survive completely alone in the wild. Over three episodes we saw Ed swimming nude, trying to shoot a squirrel out of a tree, getting frightened of bears though he never actually saw one, losing weight and crying and crying and crying."

So when the BBC asked Adam to produce four pieces for their *2009 Unwrapped* series presented by Miranda Hart, he decided to spoof Ed's dramatic video-diary style. But there was a snag. "Unfortunately my wife felt that a solo trip to Canada was an unjustifiable drain on the family finances so I decided to see how long I could survive in our shed. The shed is a very special, spiritual place for me. Because I'm one of the most famous people in the country, I am constantly hounded by paparazzi and attractive stalkers and the shed is one of the few places I can go to be free of the attention. I go there to meditate about the media (or 'media-tate'), to stare at printer boxes or just to listen to old Adam & Joe podcasts with a glass of frozen wine. I thought it would be easy to spend several weeks in there but just like Ed Wardle, I soon realised how very wrong and slightly prattish I was."

All four parts of Adam's *Alone in the Shed* video diaries can be found on YouTube.

SHED FACT

7% of men immediately head to the shed every day after they get home from work. (Though this figure may include those parking the bike.)

The Good Life - Sexual Tension In The Shed

The best-remembered scene from the movie *Ghost* features Patrick Swayze and Demi Moore and a potter's wheel. But it's 99 to 100% certain that the film-makers realised the potting wheel's potential for sexual tension by watching a similar scene in *The Good Life*. The BBC sitcom based around self-sufficiency in Surbiton featuring Richard Briers, Felicity Kendal (pictured below), Penelope Keith and Paul Eddington was watched by audiences of more than 17 million when it first went out in the 1970s.

One episode 'Going to Pot' had posh Margo attending pottery evening classes. Hen-pecked husband Jerry buys her her own shed complete with potter's wheel to practise on. But it just so happens that neighbour Tom Good turns out to be dab hand with a lump of clay and soon he and Margo are side by side, exchanging innuendo-filled dialogue in the tight confines of the Surbiton shed.

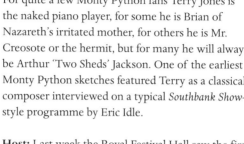

Monty Python's Arthur 'Two Sheds' Jackson

For quite a few Monty Python fans Terry Jones is the naked piano player, for some he is Brian of Nazareth's irritated mother, for others he is Mr. Creosote or the hermit, but for many he will always be Arthur 'Two Sheds' Jackson. One of the earliest Monty Python sketches featured Terry as a classical composer interviewed on a typical *Southbank Show*-style programme by Eric Idle.

Host: Last week the Royal Festival Hall saw the first performance of a new symphony by one of the world's leading modern composers, Arthur 'Two Sheds' Jackson. Mr Jackson.

Jackson: Hello.

The interviewer then goes on to ignore Arthur Jackson's large body of orchestral work and concentrate on how he got his 'Two Sheds' nickname. The irony of it being:

Jackson: No, I've only got one. I've had one for some time, but a few years ago I said I was thinking of getting another, and since then some people have called me 'Two Sheds'.

Thus starting the tradition, to be handed down from generation to generation that anybody with two sheds should be nicknamed 'Arthur Two Sheds Jackson'.

The Fast Show's Sheds

Sheds, both English and Australian, featured very heavily in the three series of *The Fast Show*. Jesse (Mark Williams) would emerge from his shed to inform the camera about his diet, with the words, "This week I 'ave mostly been eating...pop tarts". In the three series he had three different sheds to emerge from, although in the final series he veered away from food and started informing the viewer of his fashion choices, as in; "This week I 'ave been mostly wearing Dolce & Gabbana."

Bob Fleming – very much in tribute to the veteran countryman Jack Hargreaves – presented *Country Notes* from his large shed. Unlike the pipe-smoking Jack, Bob, played by Charlie Higson, can't get through a sentence without coughing, yet never realises it's that much of a problem.

Carl Hooper was an Aussie broadcaster played by Simon Day. Carl

presented the Aussie TV show *That's Amazing*, the show where members of the public bring objects to Carl's shed or tell stories which prompt the response, "That's amazing!" The trouble is none of them really are.

SHED FACT

Gustav Mahler should really have been nicknamed Gustav 'Three Huts' Mahler. Over the course of his lifetime the prolific Austrian composer built a sequence of huts. Like Edvard Grieg's they were often close to water. His first was at Steinbach near Salzburg on the Attersee. He wrote parts of Symphony No.2 and No.3 there. His second Komponierhäuschen (composition hut) was on the Wörthersee near Klagenfurt, which gave us No.5, 6, 7 and 8. His third hut at Toblach helped him create Symphonies No.9 and No.10. None inspired him to create better names for his symphonies.

Sheds *at the Movies*

Sheds don't have a big presence in the world's 100 best movies; neither Hollywood nor Bollywood accords them much screen time. In casting terms they are Pete and Dud's one-legged Tarzan, it seems all you can do with a shed is go and fetch something from it. Yet they do appear in their own right, and not just because they are central to a shed-book adaptation, such as *Kes* or *Lady Chatterley's Lover*. We have assembled some of the greatest shed movies of all time and given them their own shed rating.

Chitty Chitty Bang Bang (1968)

A children's classic, Ken Hughes and well-known shed habituee Roald Dahl based their screenplay on the original Ian Fleming novel *Chitty Chitty Bang Bang: The Magical Car*. The film depicts the familiar stereotype of the eccentric inventor, Caractacus Potts (played by Dick Van Dyke) and his equally eccentric father (Lionel Jeffries) who is mistakenly abducted by Vulgarian spies whilst pottering about in his shed – which looks suspiciously like a glammed up privvy.

Grandpa Potts and shed are airlifted across the channel to the much-loved song of the Sherman Brothers, *Posh*, whilst being dunked unceremoniously into the water. The shed and its contents, though entirely soaked, survive the ordeal. It earns its place in history as one of the only sheds in musical cinema.

As a footnote; the child catcher's wagon, into which Jeremy and Jemima are lured (serves them right), also resembles a shed.

ON SCREEN SHED TIME: 7 MINUTES.

ET The Extra Terrestrial (1982)

Another great film for kids, ET is an Ann Widdecombe-shaped alien who is busy collecting botanical samples one night when a bunch of rednecks from town arrive in the woods to find out the source of the strange lights. His spaceship promptly zooms off leaving ET behind. Left on his lonesome, the four-foot Niki Lauda lookalike hides and is foraging for food when Elliot discovers him in his garden shed. The two strike up a bond of friendship and Elliot helps ET survive and more importantly "phone home". The shed doesn't feature too strongly in the movie, but does play a pivotal role.

ON SCREEN SHED TIME: 11 MINUTES

The kind of shed that most
parents fantasise about.

Chicken Run (2000)

Aardman Animations' film showed the world that it's not just humans who scratch around in sheds. *Chicken Run* depicts a group of chickens who are imprisoned in a chicken farm, which bears a striking similarity to the POW camp depicted in *The Great Escape*. Instead of living in huts, however, the chickens live in a veritable chicken shed. The impending threat of being turned into chicken pie (and the tedium of living with a lot of other chickens) eventually drives the chickens to escape in a giant bird contraption.

ON SCREEN SHED TIME: 40 MINUTES

The Great Escape (1963)

Sheds have never been the most comfortable of living spaces especially for the Allied prisoners of war detained in Germany's state-of-the-art POW camp, Stalag Luft III. The film, based on real-life events, follows a daring plan by the prisoners to tunnel out of the camp to freedom, and, by various means, escape to safety. It's probably not giving too much away to say that Herr Bartlett ruins it.

ON SCREEN SHED TIME: 117 MINUTES.

SHED FACT

The only known print of Alfred Hitchcock's earliest feature film, *The White Shadow*, made in 1923, was found lying in a New Zealand shed for 80 years. It was found in a collection of silent movies in a shed in Hastings, North Island.

Sredni Vashtar (1981)

Andrew Birkin's Bafta-winning short film, based on the short story by Taki, examines the life of a young orphan, Conradin, who worships a ferret in his garden shed. Unbeknownst to his cruel guardian, Aunt Augusta, Conradin also has a beloved Houdan hen in the shed. When Aunt Augusta takes away the precious hen, Conradin immediately prays to his god, the shed-dwelling ferret Sredni Vashtar, and revenge is not long in coming.

ON SCREEN SHED TIME: **9** MINUTES

Gnomeo & Juliet (2011)

This lively animated adaptation of *Romeo and Juliet* casts typical garden gnomes in the eponymous roles. Far from Verona, the film is set in the back gardens of two elderly neighbours, Miss Montague and Mr. Capulet, who hate each other. The gnomes, naturally, spend most of their time pottering around in their back garden and looking like Michael Eavis.

ON SCREEN SHED TIME: **15** MINUTES

The Full Monty (1997)

This Oscar-winning comedy, set in Sheffield, stars garden gnomes, northern accents and Robert Carlyle's chest. Six unemployed men attempt to put their lives in order by forming a male striptease act, vowing to go "the full monty" and strip naked in front of their audience. In a desperate attempt to lose weight for the act, Mark Addy's character Dave locks himself in his garden shed and wraps himself in cling film. Unlike the building-your-own-spaceship-underneath-the-shed scenario, this is certainly something you can try yourself at home.

ON SCREEN SHED TIME: 1 MINUTE

The Thing (1982)

In John Carpenter's gruesome horror film, nowhere is safe, least of all the tool shed in which arctic scientists lock fellow doctor Blair (Wilford Brimley) fearing that he has been infected by an aggressive alien. Not content to bide his time, the infected Blair begins construction of a spaceship in a recess below the shed (You have to ask – who was responsible for the quality of that concrete shed base?). Helicopter pilot MacReady (Kurt Russell) guarantees it will never take off, however, by blowing it (and the sheds) to bits with a stick of dynamite.

ON SCREEN SHED TIME: 12 MINUTES

Shaun of the Dead (2004)

Edgar Wright's 2004 film not only introduced the comedic talents of Simon Pegg and Nick Frost to the big screen, but proved that a zombie can be safely stored in a shed – as long as it's got a games console for company. After learning of the zombie outbreak, Tim (Pegg) and Ed (Frost) break into their locked garden shed in search of heavy duty weaponry and settle upon a cricket bat and a spade. At the end of the film, it's revealed that Tim has been hiding his now-undead friend Ed in a shed at the bottom of his garden, a clear and certain breach of council guidelines for the Storage of Undead Friends.

ON SCREEN SHED TIME: 4 MINUTES

Speciality *Sheds*

Some sheds never get to see a rusty spade, never get to store a moth-eaten deckchair or a leaky garden hose. (One shed in Paynesville, Australia never even gets to see a garden.) For they are destined for greater things. Sheds get turned into all kinds of different edifices. There are many shed museums, quite a few shed shrines, loads of shed pubs and bars, shed cinemas, shed pirate ships, but as far as we know, just one shed wedding vehicle. *Doctor Who* fans love to build Tardis sheds, whose interiors are bound to be a disappointment. Here are just a selection of the many speciality sheds out there, all put together with an outstanding degree of originality and some big love.

Paynesville's Floating Shed

What do you do if your boat is too full of stuff? The answer – build a shed for it. This floating beauty, photographed near Paynesville on the Gippsland Lakes in the Australian state of Victoria makes an appearance on most Australia Days.

"We built it just after the floods in 2007 and it was a bit of enjoyment for the locals in the town," said shed owner and Paynesville character Bernie Smith. "I just come up with these stupid ideas. Today, everything's too serious…this is a bit of fun and it's all for nothing."

Quite often the shed can be heard before it is seen with a band entertaining townsfolk as it floats near the Paynesville wharf. "If I got a dollar for every photo taken of it, I'd be a millionaire," Mr. Smith said.

After the original floating shed was built Bernie added a floating dunny that could be towed along behind.

Splice That Apex Roof, Mr. Bosun

Amateur historian Robert Carter may only have a 12 x 6 foot shed, but that hasn't stopped him putting hundreds of historical pieces on display in one of the country's smallest museums. Retired boat builder Robert, from Plymouth, has always had a strong interest in maritime history, collecting a number of historically important items over 42 years. The exhibits on display include: a sailor's hat from the Battle of Trafalgar, coal shovels from HMS *Bulldog*, a ship's compass, a diver's torch, cutlasses, pieces of eight, a rum barrel, a powder keg and a silver admiral's whistle dated 1820.

Along with historic uniforms of naval captains, lieutenants, doctors and a mid-shipman's uniform worn by a 12-year-old boy, is a hatband from SS *Runic* made by famous British shipping company White Star Line.

With everything packed in so tightly Mr. Carter is tempted to go for bigger premises. "My ambition would be to get a decommissioned lightship put in the garden so I could turn it into a full sized museum," he told the *Daily Mail*. His wife wasn't available for comment.

The Bowling Shed

Having a home bowling alley needn't be the preserve of rock stars and football players. A ten-pin bowling fanatic in the States has installed one in an outbuilding. The Brunswick A2-automatic pinsetter is housed in his shed and when the owner wants a game, he opens the double doors and bolts on the rest of the wooden bowling lane in sections out into the garden. One of the few bowling alleys where rain stops play.

SHED FACT

It's estimated that between 5 and 6% of Britain's railway modelling takes place in a shed

▄▄▄— "Friends, Romans, Shed Owners..."

Andrew Wilkinson (Uncle Wilco) organises the Shed of the Year competition through his Shedblog. One of the early winners, in 2007, was a Roman temple erected by Tony in Berkshire.

"I remember admiring a ruined temple one year at the Chelsea Flower Show in a garden-stone display. Following on from my interest in all things Roman, I was standing at the kitchen window some time later when I casually suggested to my wife that the shed might look better if it was converted to a Roman temple."

Tony's mission was to create a folly in his back garden landscape. Many of the great country estates of England have follies that can be viewed from the main house, the only slight difference was that Tony's would be a lot closer. After three years of lobbying the missus, Tony finally took delivery of four 2.2 metre fibreglass Doric columns in 2004 and the shed/temple could begin. The finished shed includes Roman windows, murals, sculptures, a collection of amphora, a mosaic table and CCTV.

▄▄▄▟ Pirates Of The Thames Estuary

Reg Miller's pirate shed, the *Lady Sarah out of Worthing*, took Shedblog's top honour in 2010. The 16 x 8 foot standard apex shed boasts more pirate ephemera than you can shake a wooden leg at. "It's built to look like the poop deck of a pirate ship moored at a Caribbean dock. The inside of the shed is equipped with a full range of piratannical ephemera, including skulls, crossed bones (courtesy of a friendly butcher) and a dead man's chest. Outside the shed there is plenty of space for pirate roistering and carousing amongst the tropical plants and under the palm-thatched lean-to" blogged Pirate King Reg.

Showing ship's carpenter skills Reg lashed the shed together using panelled doors keelhauled out of skips and other reclaimed booty ransacked from the Southend area. Stall holders in local car boot sales got to know him so well that they used to save pirate ephemera for him.

 **Post Fan Steve**

Stephen Knight fell in love with the red British postbox about ten years ago and the love affair has flourished. Now he has 105 of them stretching from 1859 to the present day – so many in fact that he's created a museum at his house in Halstead, Essex.

The Colne Valley Postal History Museum, located in Stephen's garden, has all kinds of Royal Mail paraphernalia that would have been found in rural post offices down the years. These can be found in a self-built shed in which he has created a sub-post office. Items include stamp vending machines, balances for weighing the letters, equipment for cancelling the stamps, vendors for registered labels – everything you would find in a normal sub-post office, with the exception of moaning pensioners.

"We have one of the first wall boxes in the UK to receive letters and the design hasn't really changed since," Stephen told BBC Essex. "We also have a hexagonal Victorian postbox in the collection from 1866, but they did eventually go back to being round because it is so much easier to handle and you get a very good volume of letters for the height and space it takes up on the street."

A Few Bottles In The Shed

When Steve Wheeler's collection of milk bottles got to 150 he thought to himself that maybe it was getting a little bit out of control. Thirty years and 17,350 bottles later he still hasn't been able to curb his collecting instinct. Housed in a custom-built shed at his home in Malvern, Worcestershire, Steve's collection is one of the biggest in the world. In fact should all his milk bottles be put onto a milk lorry then the load would probably come out at around 14 tonnes.

"The most I've paid for a bottle is £150 for a nineteenth-century glass bottle that I bought from Sydney, Australia," Steve told the *Daily Mail*. "But I've probably found a few that are worth more than that by rummaging around in old barnyards. It's not just the bottles I love, it's the finding of them and the people I meet when I'm collecting them.

"The milk bottles are all completely individual – there's a fascinating history behind each and every one. They're becoming more important in terms of social history, because everyone just gets their milk in plastic or cardboard containers these days."

He was offered £80,000 for his collection but turned it down. However pretty soon he's going to need to extend the shed...

The Shiplap Odeon

Former cinema projectionist Don Parr achieved a lifetime ambition when he opened a cinema in his back garden. As a 16-year-old lad in Erdington, Birmingham in 1943 Don would switch reels at his local Apollo movie house. Now he's rescued 14 seats from a real cinema auditorium and installed them in his 18 x 9 foot garden shed, complete with movie posters and all the decor from a classic 1930s venue.

"It's a real blast from the past because it's decked out in a very nostalgic way," Don told the *Daily Telegraph*, "I think I did it because I just love the way films can affect people when they see them, it's just magical to watch sometimes."

He's been working on his cinema project with two friends since 1987 and when the curtain first raised, it was two 16mm projectors providing the entertainment. Now, the background noise has been considerably reduced by using a big screen LCD and a Blu-ray player. Interval ice creams are available, but only in the summer months.

Forget The Bentley, I Ordered A Shed

Newlywed Sara Scott emerged from Horsford church in Norfolk unsure what vehicle would be taking her to the reception. Her groom, Tristan Scott, had been suitably vague about the means of transport in the months before the wedding. When she walked out of the church she found a beautifully decorated white shed, complete with sofa, waiting on the back of a trailer for her. She should have suspected – Tristan runs a shed company.

Neath's American Diner

Paul Siudowski from Neath in South Wales transformed his 10 x 8 foot garden shed into a 1950s American time machine (pictured right). And he enjoyed what he'd built so much he extended it to 16 feet long. Like Stephen Knight and Steve Wheeler, Paul used a shed to express his collecting instinct. He and his wife have been collecting American memorabilia for the past 20 years. The wooden structure in his back garden is packed with Americana, a jukebox and decorated like a 1950s diner that even The Fonz would feel comfortable in. "What makes it really special is the fact that from the outside it just looks like a normal shed," says Paul, "everyone is absolutely amazed when they open the doors." And like the B52's single *Love Shack*, Paul also has a car "as big as a whale" but it's a 1957 Chevrolet, not a Chrysler.

The shed's gonna get you!

SHED FACT

The shed is a much-feared object in Slavic folklore, acting as the home of Baba Yaga, a witchlike character who flies around on a giant pestle kidnapping children. Baba Yaga's shed also happens to stand on giant chicken's legs. The story may be based on a Ukrainian tradition of cutting off a group of three or four trees growing close together and using their stumps as a base for a shed.

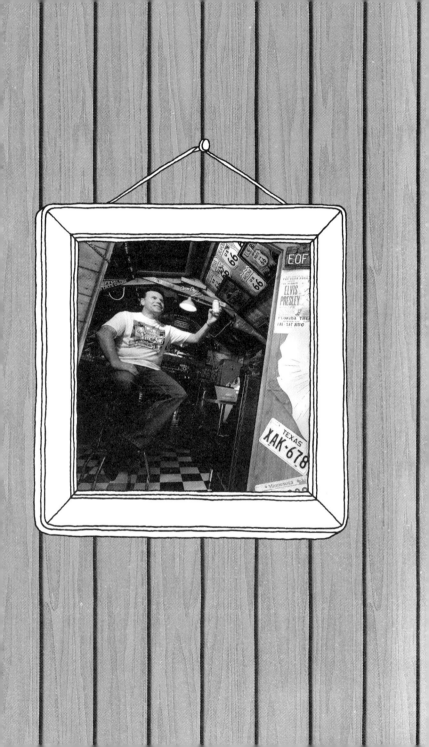

Shed *Imposters*

Such is the lure of the shed that these days many businesses and venues want to be associated with shed chic. There is something about the rough, no-nonsense nature of a shed that they aspire to. Either that or they like to bask in the brilliant wit of calling a multi-million pound structure a shed. Here are just some of the many shed imposters that aren't based in a shed and where there isn't a shiplap panel in sight.

The Music Shed Recording Studios

LOCATION: New Orleans, Louisiana

ACTUAL BUILDING: Bricks and mortar state of the art recording studios.

VERDICT: New Orleans is the home of trad jazz and it's certainly safe to say that trad jazz belongs in a shed, preferably one with extensive sound-proofing.

The Shed End, Chelsea FC

LOCATION: West London

ACTUAL BUILDING: Large concrete and steel grandstand, replacing an older grandstand that looked a bit like a shed – if you can have such a thing as a two-tiered shed. Unless of course they were talking about the groundsman's shed behind it.

VERDICT: The unacceptable face of football shed hooliganism.

The Shed Bar

LOCATION: Leeds

ACTUAL BUILDING: Bricks and mortar hostelry located underneath a railway arch.

VERDICT: Might be excused if they inserted the word 'railway' into the title.

M Shed

LOCATION: Bristol

ACTUAL BUILDING: State of the art, steel, glass and concrete museum.

VERDICT: Sounds funkier than Bristol Industrial Museum – which is essentially what it was until 2006.

It may look like a shed, but it's not. The Shed End terrace at Chelsea F.C., pictured here in 1965 as major groundwork got underway at Stamford Bridge, with several pie stalls replaced. All that is left of the terrace today is some beautifully preserved concrete. Not exactly Pompeii.

The Potting Shed Pub

LOCATION: The Cotswolds, between Tetbury, Malmesbury and Cirencester.

ACTUAL BUILDING: Bricks and mortar.

VERDICT: It may have been voted Dining Pub of the Year 2011, and it may have started all manner of innovative fruit and veg schemes, but it's still not based in a potting shed. We need to see 40% of the internal floor space devoted to seedlings and sundry horticultural-based activities before we'll accept shed.

The Bed Shed

LOCATION: Thirty-six branches through Scotland and north-east England.

ACTUAL BUILDING: Bricks and mortar, concrete and steel retail units.

VERDICT: This bed retailer is trading on the shed's ability to rhyme with its principal sales product, plus the inference that because it's a no-frills structure you're likely to get a good deal.

Sunglasses Hut

LOCATION: Gatwick, Heathrow and Stansted Airports.

ACTUAL BUILDING: Concrete and steel retail unit.

VERDICT: If you're stupid enough to pay high prices for branded products when you can get a pretty decent copy off an itinerant Senegalese trader at the tourist destination of your choice, then go ahead.

The Bike Shed Theatre

LOCATION:	Exeter
ACTUAL BUILDING:	A basement below The Bike Shed Shop.
VERDICT:	This is unlikely to last long. Presumably there are only so many plays you can write about bike sheds.

The Bike Shed Shop

LOCATION:	Exeter
ACTUAL BUILDING:	A bricks and mortar shop above the Bike Shed Theatre.
VERDICT:	Try parking your bike there overnight and see how friendly they are.

Shed Media

LOCATION:	Gray's Inn Road, London.
ACTUAL BUILDING:	Bricks and mortar building for a television company that produces a whole stream of well-known series including *Supernanny*, *Garrow's Law*, *Waterloo Road* and *Who Do You Think You Are?*
VERDICT:	Who do they think they are naming themselves after a no-nonsense household outbuilding and probably having expensive lunches at The Ivy…?

Sensible Shed Talk
from the 1950s

"Hoi, you there with that cheap garden building catalogue! Why don't you get out your gimlet and mortice gauge and make one yourself?" From the golden age of sheds, we bring you some sensible tips and hints about how to construct your own garden building, and how to avoid the creeping shoddiness of the inferior purchased outhouse. No dovetail joints are required to build our medley of garden buildings.

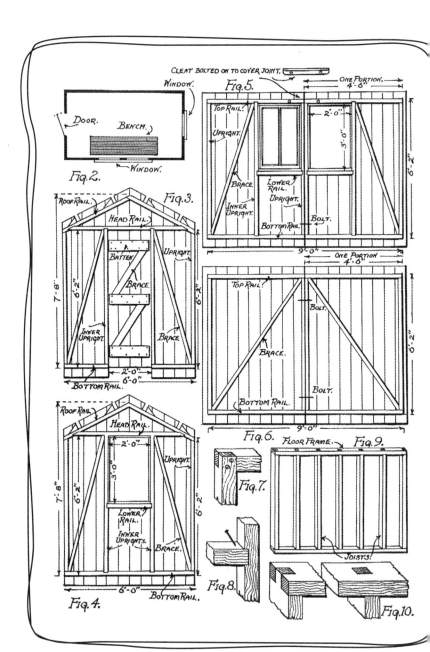

CLEAT BOLTED ON TO COVER JOINT.

WINDOW.

DOOR.   BENCH.

WINDOW.

Fig. 2.

Fig. 5.

ONE PORTION.
4'-6"

TOP RAIL.

UPRIGHT.

2'-0"

3'-0"

6'-2"

BRACE.   LOWER RAIL.
UPRIGHT.

INNER UPRIGHT.

BOTTOM RAIL.   BOLT.

Fig. 3.

ROOF RAIL.

HEAD RAIL.

BATTEN.

UPRIGHT.

BRACE.

7'-8"   6'-2"   6'-2"

INNER UPRIGHT.   BRACE.

2'-0"
6'-0"

BOTTOM RAIL.

9'-0"
ONE PORTION
4'-6"

TOP RAIL.

BOLT.

6'-2"

BRACE.

BOTTOM RAIL.   BOLT.

9'-0"

Fig. 6.

FLOOR FRAME.   Fig. 9.

Fig. 4.

ROOF RAIL.

HEAD RAIL.

2'-0"

3'-0"

UPRIGHT.

7'-8"   6'-2"   6'-2"

LOWER RAIL.

INNER UPRIGHTS.   BRACE.

6'-0"   BOTTOM RAIL.

Fig. 7.

Fig. 8.

JOISTS.

Fig. 10.

Garden Woodwork

Gardening and woodwork invariably go together. Most of the structures required in the garden are made wholly or partly of wood, and the man who is handy with tools can save himself a great deal of expense by making things for himself. Apart from this, however, he will get a tremendous amount of fun out of it, with the added advantage of making things exactly to the size and style to suit himself. It is, of course, necessary to have somewhere to work, and a garden workshop should be considered as an early item to put in hand. In the meantime it will probably be necessary to work in the garage, outhouse, or in any other temporary place. The important thing is to have a cover where timber, etc. can be kept until the workshop itself is available.

There are all sorts of things that the amateur wood-worker can make for garden or outdoor use and by doing so one can achieve a considerable saving on costs. Things such as plant tubs, flower boxes, seats, gates and the like are not so difficult to make as at first they may appear, and apart from the saving in outlay, the work of constructing them is congenial and satisfying. Much of this satisfaction is derived from the process of designing the items and to this end the projects discussed in this chapter are intended as a guide or pointers to enable the reader to devise his own design, based on his individual requirements.

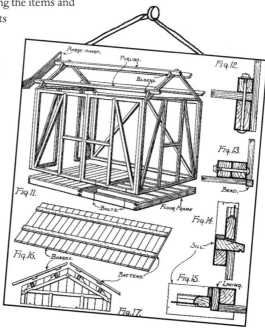

Beach Or Garden Chalet

Those who are lucky enough to have a small plot of land on the coast may have thought of a beach chalet where they can take their families for holidays and weekends, without incurring hotel or boarding-house expenses. What a delight it would be to awaken so close to the seashore. Fig. I shows a portable building which can be used in the garden when not in use at the coast. It is important to stress that proximity to the sea and abrasive salty air will require a rigorous programme of maintenance which must be adhered to if the building is not to succumb to rapid dilapidation. Strong wind will also necessitate that cladding and roof are applied with the strongest of fixations.

FIG. I. DUAL-PURPOSE CHALET
This versatile design would serve well as an ordinary garden shed or workshop, and, with the added feature of the veranda, could form an attractive garden chalet. With slight alterations to sizes, it would also make an ideal cricket pavilion

Tool Shed

Wherever a garden or allotment is cultivated a tool shed is a necessity. In the majority of cases it is impossible to find room within the dwelling-house to store the necessary tools and appliances required in the cultivation of the home-garden, as, in addition to forks, spades, and such-like tools, a lawn mower, and perhaps a small roller have to be accommodated. Similarly, when an allotment is being cultivated there is no task so irksome as having to carry the tools forward and back. Even more than in the home-garden, a shelter from an occasional storm, and a seat on which to rest is very desirable.

The tool shed shown and described below is suitable for the garden or the allotment and may be adapted to meet individual needs. For the home garden some care should be taken with the selection of material and the workmanship, so that the shed may conform with its surroundings. Wood must, of course, be used for the framework. Matched or weather-boarding, if obtainable, may be used for covering, but asbestos cement sheets make a good substitute, while corrugated sheets could be used for covering the roof.

For the allotment, a wood-framed shed, covered even with galvanised iron, answers the purpose quite adequately. It is advisable to fit a small window in the back of the shed, and it will be beneficial to the garden and its crops if means are taken to collect the rain-water draining from the roof of the shed.

Shed For Cycle Or Pram

Many cycle sheds are expensive to construct, being planned to a size which permits a person to enter when the cycle is placed within. Here is shown a type so built that the cycle or pram is wheeled in while the owner remains outside. If erected against a wall, or preferably where two walls meet, the saving in timber is considerable.

The shed is made with a door at the end for the entry of the cycle (or pram), and the machine is controlled and placed in the rest by opening a flap which is provided at the top of the side. For a single cycle the shed should be 6 ft. long by 4ft. 3 in. high by 2 ft. wide. For two cycles it must be proportionately wider, for a tandem slightly longer. For a pram only a small building is necessary according to the type in use.

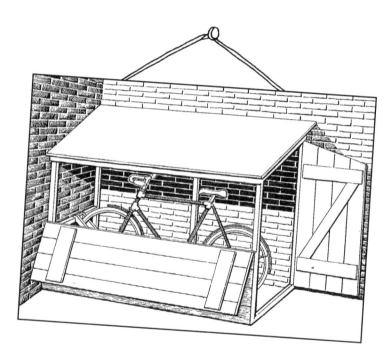

Wood-framed, Asbestos-covered Garage

When building a garage, it is always advisable to consider what one's future requirements may be, for many motorists are not always satisfied with the smaller type of car, and it is most annoying, when purchasing a larger car, to find that the garage is not large enough for it. The extra space of a larger garage will always come in handy, whether to accommodate a work bench or to provide storage space for trunks, luggage or any other sundry items that may be inconvenient to store in a loft.

➤ Lean-to Shed

If only the lawn mower has to be accommodated, the shed may be as small as 1ft. 6in. square on plan, but if a mower and roller have to be sheltered in the shed it will have to be as large again.